1

Oliver Mayer

Collected Plays:

(Where the Music Is)

NoPassport Press

Front cover photo: from Black Dahlia Theater's production of *Ragged Time*. Courtesy of Black Dahlia Theater. Back cover photo of author courtesy of Andrew Furnevel.

First edition 2007 by NoPassport Press
PO Box 1786, South Gate CA 90280 USA

NoPassport Press
Dreaming the Americas Series

Series Editors: Caridad Svich, Jorge Huerta, Otis Ramsey-Zoe

Advisory Board: Daniel Banks, Maria M. Delgado, Amparo Garcia-Crow, Randy Gener, Elana Greenfield, Saviana Stanescu, Sarah Cameron Sunde, Tamara Underiner.

NoPassport Press is a division of NoPassport an unincorporated international theatre alliance founded in 2001 by Caridad Svich devoted to diversity, difference and freedom of expression in theatre arts. For more information about NoPassport and/or this print series contact NoPassportPress@aol.com

ISBN: 978-0-6151-8370-1
$19.95 paperback.

3

Contents

Acknowledgments:

The author would like to thank the following people and organizations for their support and encouragement:

Howard Stein, Columbia, playwriting mentor and spiritual godfather
Jon Stallworthy, Cornell, who showed me the rigor of poetry, and the beauty
Dean Madeline Puzo, and the entire USC School of Theatre
Velina Hasu Houston, cherished colleague and friend
Luis Alfaro, colleague, friend and El Lay brother
Jon Lawrence Rivera, artistic director of Playwrights Arena, Los Angeles
Alfonso Arau, *mas chingon que la chingada*
Tony Kelly, artistic director of Thick Description, San Francisco
Alice Romano and The Independent Writers of Southern California
Randy Reinholz and Native Voices at the Autry
John Ortiz and The LAByrinth Theatre
David Roman, USC professor, mentor and friend
Jon Rossini, UC Davis, esteemed colleague
Caridad Svich, friend, colleague and visionary
Jorge Huerta, UCSD, professional and spiritual guide, and dear friend
Bill Nericcio, SDSU, professor extraordinaire, Chicano activist, and brother
Angus Fletcher, USC blood brother
Paula Holt, producer and lover of theatre
Gordon Davidson, who gave me my start in many ways
Natsuko Ohama, velvet-voiced comrade
Jack Rowe, director, teacher and guitar picker extraordinaire
Alan Mayer, brother
Keith Coleman, brother
Gloria Mayer, mother and source of constant inspiration
Marlene Forte, who I've been waiting for all my life

And to the memory of:
Ron Link
Alexander A. Mayer
Balder and Pistolino
And Nature Boy

This book is *para mi mas roja flama*

Preface

The L.A. Sound

Boxing is a good metaphor for Oliver Mayer. He loves the fights and he loves that a great boxer in the ring can also be a great ballet dancer. At its most primal, a flailing body in the ring going all twelve rounds can become a piece of music. And music plays an essential role in an Oliver Mayer play. His plays have a melody, a tempo, a rhythm that few writers possess. Plays like *Young Valiant*, *Joe Louis Blues*, *Ragged Time* and *Joy of the Desolate*. Poetic, full of heart, the aching of characters longing to connect with one another, and with the city. This is the place that I believe Oliver Mayer writes from – he listens to the soundtrack of a city - its people - and he hears their song. He has uncanny ability to translate people's needs into poetry. His plays resonate musically because they are full of jazz riffs and soliloquies that become full of a character's inner rhythm and, yes - song. Characters in his plays, don't just speak – they seem to sing their stories.

Last year (2006) I had the pleasure of listening to the literal music of an Oliver Mayer play in a piece that he created for his wife and partner, Marlene Forte, called *Rocio! In Spite of it All*, a hilarious and tragic musical about celebrity that was staged in a club on Hollywood Boulevard. Even when his characters sing they sound like poets. But back to boxing for a moment...

Beside the obvious extraordinary years of his success with a boxing play called *Blade to the Heat*, which had great runs both in New York at The Public Theater and here in L.A. at the Mark Taper Forum, Oliver has been putting up the good fight for a long time. And by the good fight, I mean – committing himself to that act of solitude that we call - writing.

The life of a playwright is: one half monk and one half party hostess. You have to dig deep into your soul and find the quiet lonely place where you confront your deepest darkest fears, hopes and you connect them to a question that you have about the world. If we are lucky, that question turns into an obsession – that haunts our dreams - and turns into a thesis - that turns into a theatrical idea that becomes your lover for a year. And then you give it away to a director – who hopefully completes the *ménage a trois* of creativity in a good way. And finally you join the party of a production, trying to cast all the players in the best effort to give birth to your baby.

I used to wonder what playwrights and directors did off in the corner whispering to each other like an old married couple. After my first production, I realized that they are talking about that baby you have been carrying around for nine months, trying to figure out how to introduce it to the world. So, the mark of a great playwright is not in what I call Oliver's

Blade to the Heat period where he was deservedly running off to New York, Chicago and Mexico City celebrating his great play. That's just one of the fun perks of having a hit play.

No, the mark of a great playwright is in that period where no one is paying attention to what you are doing. That place - post *Next Great Thing* and *Everybody Stopped Giving A Shit*, where the phone stops ringing, the email inquiries don't I.M. and the mail box is empty. That amazing place where all you have is the canvas that is the empty page, the pen and your desire. A quiet lonely place where we begin to dream for the sake of dreaming. That's the place where a playwright not only gets his characters – he builds a character for himself. Oliver has created great characters – and in the process – made a great character of himself. In boxing terms – he keeps stepping back into the ring.

He's been consistently produced for the last fifteen years. In fact, last year, Playwrights Arena in Los Angeles presented a wonderful production of one Oliver's best plays, *Conjunto*, as part of its season. A beautiful play about the Japanese community in Los Angeles and the tragedy of the Internment Camps during World War II. But this wasn't just a play about history. It was a play about the tensions between Japanese and Latinos, and in a typical *Mayer-esque* quality, about the commonalities that these communities share as well. It's a typical Oliver Mayer play in that the people in his plays look like the people that live in Los Angeles. In fact, in all of his plays, his worlds are inhabited by something beautiful and real – a cast of characters that give voice to this City so dangerously perched by the ocean at the end of the world. This city of great possibility.

More and more the American Theater has been become the theater of nostalgia - the revival - a place that has stopped celebrating today and now only looks backward for its vision of the future. In Oliver's plays, everybody looks like us. And somehow, that makes his plays forward. L.A. with its 10 million inhabitants and over 150 languages should look like a new world and in Oliver's plays they do.

Maybe that's why I have come to love him and his work – I always see some part of who we are or how we dream. But the fact that I love the most is that Oliver has made a commitment to Los Angeles. He lives this city, he breathes this city and he writes about this city.

It takes a great writer to make great work.

It takes a great character to bring it to life.

Oliver you are a great character.

Luis Alfaro

Los Angeles, CA; July 2007

The Music of History

For Oliver Mayer, the subject is history. This statement resonates in multiply powerful ways in the plays in this collection: *Ragged Time*, *Joe Louis Blues*, and *Conjunto*. Combined, these works illuminate an aesthetic project invested in the recuperation and dramatization of increasingly color-full U.S. histories. Like August Wilson, Mayer employs a historical lens to generate a sense of life in two moments—the play's time and our own; the chronological distance offers a glimpse into alternative ways of being in the world and fosters the possibility of defamiliarizing human relationships. At the same time his subjects are themselves reconceptualizing their own identity through the use of music as a means of crafting community and individual performances of self. Mayer's investment in characters (dis)placed by structures of power and institutionalized rhetoric allies his work with progressive politics that insist on expanding the cultural imagination of American identity and history to explore both the indignant horror and the joy that are a part of being human. Music, the paradoxically ineffable and material performance of sound, is both atmospheric, helping to set the history of the space, and transcendent, temporarily lifting the characters past the limits of their material circumstances. This doubled function helps clarify the sense of both/and, the ruthless desire for more that

Mayer's characters keep believing they can, and should, want. Music as an idea can come dangerously close to reification as a stereotype of culture, a historical fixity or trap that keeps the characters in (their) place. Music as taste becomes a safe way to articulate division when charged terms of race must be avoided. And yet, part of Mayer's power is reminding his readers, and more importantly his listeners, that when the music is playing all bets are off—music functions as an different kind of articulation of a body against the weight of history.

Situated during moments of international conflict—the Spanish-American War and World War II—these plays provide an oblique lens to examine cultural turning points through individual human engagements inflected by the political and social conditions in which they manifest. They offer a complex glimpse into the self-fashioning of men within conflicted cultural spaces since one story that consistently surfaces in the work is a masculine *bildungs roman*, a coming into one's own, an act of self-making that defiantly punctuates the continued manifestation of identity. Being a man in Mayer's work is a combination of style and compromise, of maturation through the possibility of a performative reframing of the self. Like Luis Valdez's *Zoot Suit*, Mayer writes a combination of "fact and fantasy," sharing his enthusiasm for the energy that emerges from the ironies of the real—historical "facts" that resonate with the power of fiction. By situating these plays within heightened moments of cultural transition and the looming threat of personal and nationally sanctioned aggression, Mayer catalyzes an awareness of potential and real violence contained in the weight of cultural history. Mayer's work here creates new spaces for the articulation of Chicano playwrights, disrupting the easy assumption that a Chicano play is made visible by facile attention to the surface quality of its subject—the identity of its characters. Instead, Mayer places that easy assumption in question—not to dismiss it but rather to expand his thinking through of cultural assumptions about identity, masculinity, and representation that haunt the plays. Dealing with issues of identity in racialized rather than ethnic terms, Mayer highlights the ambivalent histories that illustrate the negotiation between U.S. self-presentation and the lived experience of individuals exposed to the economic, cultural, and personal violence that sustains conventional representation. His plays suggest the possibility there is a different way of doing history, a different way of telling stories, that comes not from a specific style of music but from the performance of music itself in relation to one's own embodied history.

Ragged Time, set in 1898 at the moment of the Spanish-American War, the second major constructed military engagement of the expansionist

U.S. 19th century (along with the Mexican-American War) echoes the

fictional history E.L. Doctorow's novel *Ragtime* (set in a later historical

moment), William Saroyan's sense of the shifting atmosphere of daily life in

the shadow of war or its possibility, and most importantly, the fundamental

messiness of temporality itself. Premiered at 2002 at Black Dahlia Theatre

in Los Angeles, *Ragged Time* has also been presented at the Royal Court

Theatre New American Play Festival in London (along with full-length

works by playwrights Quincy Long and Caridad Svich) and the Taper New

Works Festival. While Abe, the Russian Jewish immigrant newspaper

vendor is the only character explicitly conscious of the conflict in Cuba, the

specter of a hemispheric and increasingly global U.S. empire is one of the

jagged visibilities of this temporality. However, *Ragged Time* is set in a

conceptual geography, a Charleston in a "Deep South of the Mind," that

enables the possibility of embodying the weight of history. The characters

are not types, but Mayer, through his effective use of specific vernacular,

articulates his characters as at least partially in the 19th century, not as a

product of setting but as a question of style—they are implicitly engaged in a

dialogue with their own 19th century representations—melodramatic types

they simultaneously reference and question. This doubleness is manifest in

the shared contemporary understanding of the cultural weight of racial identification in the south—we must accept the weight of history, but what that acceptance means is a rough suture at best.

Reminding his audience of Charleston's role as an epicenter of the violent commodification of human beings through the institutionally sanctioned practice of slavery, Mayer implicates us within this history by staging the too familiar question of a color line—a blind black musician cannot be led by a boy physically lighter than himself, nor can he be seen spending time with a mulatta prostitute passing for white. Mayer troubles our visually saturated model of perception through the two black men in the play, both blind, both musicians, and connected in a troubled patrilineal relationship—Gary once served as Ross's boy. Gary negotiates the world through smell—his blindness becomes a source of income enhancing the generative power of his music with the possibility of charity for his performed abjection as a poor, blind man. Gary, wealthy enough to buy the young Mexican musician Ignacio from Freda, is cheated by reliance on another's sight and his own stereotypes vis-à-vis Mexican identity—Ignacio is neither strong nor dark. Freda's choice to sell Ignacio is later narrated by White Shadow, a patronizing paternal figure of white racist colonialism, as a sign of the ease with which the practice of slavery consistently re-emerges as a means of securing own's one place in the world.

Ignacio, as a child, is subject to the desires of those around him—a potential allegory of Mexico as a space for representational manipulation in the increasing complex racial landscape of U.S. politics. Ignacio's anachronistic presence is a sign not only of the raggedness of history, but a reminder that his negotiation for autonomy and struggle for identity is not a historical subject. His choice to re-enter a role as Gary's boy exemplifies the ragged shaping of our own personal histories. As his talents spread from the piano to a cartoon ukulele, Ignacio demonstrates the power of music to transform not only the self, but a larger social space, affecting even the two-dimensional characters from the funny papers. While Ignacio ultimately rejects this two-dimensional fictionality, the living funny papers not only stage the power of yellow journalism that birthed and nurtured the shared patriotic vigor of a deliberately distorted memory—"Remember the Maine"—but also suggest both the flatness of representational stereotypes and recharacterize the possibility of reinvention and social mobility known as the "American dream."

Abe and Ignacio, the immigrant and the orphan son of immigrants, are the only characters who voice the potentially optimistic model of a traditional American dream, but the play, while not denying this possibility, insists that moving forward requires displacing white colonialist attitudes (the knockout of White Shadow) and shifting or silencing the representational distortion of the press (Shadow's body is covered in a shroud of newspapers). The cartoonish stereotypes remind us that while transformation exists and can happen, the fiction of being completely free from the weight of history and cultural memory is not only a fantasy, it is the first step in a self-distorted emotionally empty life. The future manifests through music—Ignacio comes into his own as a musician in a style that comes from his people, a concept that Mayer invokes inclusively. Rather than a biological or limited cultural genealogy, Ignacio's music is the product of his life, of the intersecting cultures and traditions that make up the loose and frayed threads of the play's history.

Joe Louis Blues and *Conjunto* move us to a different historical moment of the nation at war—the early 1940's. The complex narratives on the home front and in the combat zones of World War II offer the irony of a morally justified military intervention practiced by an institutionally racist nation. Tragically, the European beaches, forests and fields and Pacific island jungles became the site of a new argument about the inclusion of African Americans, Japanese Americans, and Mexican Americans into full cultural citizenship, an argument made by the sacrifice of young males. Mayer's plays, though set in the home front, explore this tension of one's right to be a citizen and to simply be.

Like Mayer's best known play, *Blade to the Heat*, *Joe Louis Blues* reflects the playwright's fascination with boxing based on his autobiographical experience as a teenager. Premiered by Thick Description (San Francisco) in 2000, it was also produced at the Tiffany Theatre (Los Angeles) in 2001. The play's title calls to mind both the troubling wartime experiences of the champion boxer and the songs created to honor him. As a means of exploring issues of identification and self-determination in the black community Mayer employs two iconic historical figures, Sidney Bechet and Joe Louis Barrow, simultaneously humanizing them and insisting on their greatness within their specific field of endeavor—blues and boxing. Louis—an unrepentant womanizer operating according to his own moral code but anxious to do the right thing—is manipulated by his own patriotism and the War department into a fiscal crisis that he is prevented from resolving. In his role as populist hero Louis is both a symbol and a catalyst for the transformation of Demas Dean, the young blues musician whose incomplete sense of self is hidden by a combination of naïve aggressiveness and awe. Demas' acquiescence to Joe's desires to spend time with his girl Leila is an ironic parallel to the destructive elements of Joe's own submission to national needs. Here Mayer draws attention to the way that specific cultural moments and manipulations by those in power shift what might otherwise function as self-less acts.

Demas' story, the cornet player who comes into his own as a man, moves between his idealization of Joe Louis as a sign of the possibility of transcendence and his matured celebration of Joe Louis as a man worthy of respect. Demas' coming into his manhood is aided by the practical wisdom of Sidney Bechet, a master musician of a previous era who never received the attention he deserved. Mayer's play provides the additional pleasure of the re-presentation of this genius. Leila's movement from Demas to Joe and beyond plays with the conventional narrative of employing physical attractiveness as a means of progress because she is propelled in this way not by herself, but by the men around her. Initially caught up in the fantasy of Joe as icon, she is capable of shifting into the role of social climber as Joe first supports her and then silently passes her on to Barney, the Jewish impresario. The low point of Leila's self-performance is her willingness to bleach her skin in order to move beyond the spaces of Harlem. She wants to move downtown, to be on the radio and in the movies, and is willing to do what is necessary, but this attempt to chemically bleach her identity is abandoned in a moment of self-recognition and her power as a woman is never compromised. Importantly, maturation for Mayer precludes the possibility of maudlin self-pity and the potentially melodramatic moments of his work never slip into that mode.

Though she capitulates to the path of her social climb, Leila initially refuses to give in to the men's demands that she sing the blues. While she is capable of doing so, she sees the blues as a cultural capitulation, smiling in the face of pain as a means of disguising and displacing it. Instead, she maintains the power of her anger as a way of sustaining herself—not working through it by performing the blues. Her refusal serves as a powerful reminder of the way that cultural forms are reified into stereotypical forms even as they retain their cultural power and importance. The blues become an ambiguous signifier subject to problematic gestures mediated between representation and pragmatism. Mayer carefully scripts the complexities of minstrelized performances of blackness through the voice of Barney. Critiquing Leila for not only refusing the blues but for singing a racist song, something that is unacceptable both for her and for the liberally enlightened space of his club, especially because of the commercial appeal of his progressive black performers, he claims the authority to articulate what constitutes an acceptable black identity. This ostensible liberalism is countered by Sidney's performance of the same song as a way of reaching out and establishing an emotional connection with Leila in a demonstration for Demas. Like Charles Fuller's *A Soldier's Play*, Mayer carefully articulates a range of possible black identities, questioning the institutional and representational pressure to pin and preserve such an identity.

Music becomes the space through which this ambivalence is negotiated through a pragmatic recognition of the transcendence of music and the limitations placed upon by institutions, audiences, and occasionally even the performers themselves. Sidney's account of calling his dog Goolah serves multiple purposes in highlighting this tensive but productive relationship between identity and music. Insisting on the power of music to call someone, he simultaneously locates the power of this calling through an oblique reference to the creolized African cultures of the Atlantic coast, inverting Vantyle's hierarchical critique of regional difference with black culture that deploys "geechee" as a sign of a lack of sophistication. Vantyle's own Caribbean origins are mentioned by Demas and this regional tension is a part of the performance of difference and the attempt to assert or erase forms of "authentic blackness" that are paralleled with a sense of maturation and responsibility. In a sense, an acceptance of the complexity of one's own position is the end of this play, even as Vantyle himself offers an alternative—the performance of success in the face of utter destruction, the need to front, to be able to tell a story of success in the face of failure.

The difficulties and complexities of self-knowledge are encapsulated in Sidney's neologism—"incognegro." Initially presented as advice to Demas to stay invisible in the face of the military draft for World War II, the term racially marks the space of concealment and hiding. Becoming "without knowledge" and invisible is directly tied to the racialized self that Leila attempts to erase in her confusion over her own identity. However, this built in ambivalence and implicit self-hiding is not intended as simply a critique of the conditions of racism that make the possibility of authentic self-knowledge that much more difficult, but rather a sign of the ambivalent possibilities of the icon. In the face of what appears to be Joe's failure/betrayal, Demas, the one man most directly impacted by Joe's choices, stands up for what he did, what was done, and refuses to reduce the man to one event or to the machinations and manipulations of others histories and agendas.

Like *Joe Louis Blues* and *Ragged Time*, *Conjunto* both tells a new story about a historical moment and uses the specific weight and limits of that history to illustrate the complexities of relationships and self-articulation. Returning to the more familiar Chicano space of California agriculture serves to highlight the sometimes forgotten complexity of the experience of agricultural labor during World War II. The play premiered in 2003 at Teatro Visión (San José, CA), was reworked and produced at Borderlands Theater (Tucson) in 2006 followed by a production later that year at Playwrights' Arena (Los Angeles). *Conjunto* deals specifically with the crossovers of marginalization, with the effects of the Japanese internment camps on the fracturing both of the Japanese and the Asian American community. Finding a middle ground at the close of the play means renegotiating the gaps of ethnicity based on an ethic of hard work that enables individuals to do as they want, and as they must, regardless of the opportunities they are provided within the space of pre and post World War II U.S. culture.

Conjunto, the music of the borderlands, reflects a complex cultural working class heritage, but also suggests the conjoining, the ensemble itself that is necessary for the advancement of all of the people involved in this creative enterprise. Though *conjunto* music is not central to the play, historical popular music and Min's desire to be one of the "Oriental Inkspots" serves as a means of charting the multiple effects of family tradition and expectation as well as externalized racialized assumptions about authentic performance and the limits of racial difference that consistently protects the category of American as a white category. Music becomes a means of moving through and crossing over—music enables an alternative possibility of being in the world. It also becomes a means of negotiating community as the shared songs of labor both create community and chart the changes in that community's constitution as the languages and tunes shift to reflect an increasing reliance on Mexican labor.

Min, Shoko, and even Pichuka point to the real importance of having the right to engage in a cultural performance that may not be one's "own." The very concept of "own" is at stake in Mayer's play in which the essentially forced sale of the Yamada property places the economic sense of the term in question and where the hybridization of life practices at the intersection of Mexican, Japanese, and U.S. identities. Ted's recognition of a connection with Pichuka, the pachuca who offers a counter to the *campesino* figure Genevevo, begins the process of racialized crossing and affiliations that questions categories assumed to be isolated and oppositional. Adopting an often comic relationship to the act of crossing over, Pichuka nonetheless is "educated" into the possibility of a minimal distance between pachuco and *campesino* while simultaneously bridging the gaps with Japanese culture. The distance between Shoko and Min illustrates the distance between recent immigrants and assimilated ethnic Americans, and the problems that emerge when both of these identities become overly rigid in their manifestation. The possibility of self-transformation is most powerfully staged in Shoko's act of becoming a worker. Placing the traditionally humble garb on her body is accompanied by Mayer's indication of a sense of harmony and dignity, not only celebrating the importance of labor but also suggesting the possibility of a meaningful and authentic sense of crossing cultures.

Shoko's shared dream illustrates the representational difficulties inherited by the substitution of popular culture for traditional spiritualities, a humorous exploration that engages meaningfully with a search for the self predicated on something beyond everyday experience. Her invocation of Gene Autry and Jorge Negrete as gods demonstrates not only the difficulty of creating figures that can serve as models, but the representational influence of the big screen and the literal transformation into gods that occurs because of the epic scope of both the narratives and the images of these icons. Like Demas Dean's fascination with Joe Louis, Min and Genevevo articulate their identities through these figures of western masculinity. The screen heroes' failure to offer a solution to Shoko's identity crisis reflects not only the complexity of her situation but also the difficulty of reflecting real complexity in everyday life, where Asian identities are conflated and contained and where an air raid emerges from hysteria.

The play's resolution following Min's return from the internment camp is crucial—Shoko destroys the capitalistic medium of exchange, the dollars she is given and invokes a coming together of the two men, Min who is coming back to what he once owned, and Genevevo who both was given and usurped authority over the place in addition to garnering Shoko's affection. Her gesture of reconciliation contains a powerful theatrical element, calling them back together in a way that makes them one—Yamada and *llamada*—an act of naming and a call that gesture towards the possibility of sameness through the homonymic status of the language, even as the reader of the text can see a difference between the statements. The end of *Conjunto* calls for a new social order, a new creative ensemble, one never fully capable of realization, but one that can manifest on the Yamada farm, a space of growth and transformation.

In these three plays Mayer sets up a way of thinking with and through history to gesture towards alternatives that, fictional though they may be, gain the resonance of possibilities always immanent, reminding the reader and the audience that the narratives and the weight of our own histories, though not imaginary, invisible or without power, are narratives. History shapes the process of self-discovery and maturation even as the very nature of that history is questioned. Music becomes a way of crossing over, reflecting a different means of performing the self through establishing the ability to communicate *as* a definition of self rather than the need to communicate a specific version *of* a sense of self. Mayer offers, through his music, both instrumental and linguistic sonorities, the possibility of other ways of seeing, ways of reclaiming and reimagining icons, of developing authentic selves and relationships in the face of divisive structures of power.

Jon D. Rossini

University of California-Davis

September 2007

"Where the music is…"

was the catchphrase of KNX FM, a Los Angeles radio station from the 1970s. As a child, I would sit in the backseat of my mother's Peugeot listening to the DJ speak, followed by the songs of Cat Stevens, Joni Mitchell, and a host of pop folk troubadours who effortlessly taught me nuance and story, history and harmony, sex appeal and heartbreak.

Perhaps I began writing plays in those moments, because I felt not only my own heart beating but the hearts of others, fantasies of exotic lives lived out in sound images neither completely in the present or the past but somewhere in concentrated time and space.

Years later, in a true epiphany only partially derived by stimulants, I saw the notes of a Bach toccata I was listening to on the stereo somehow swirl around me in a visible double helix only to slowly separate literally into thin air.

Perhaps the helix first formed itself in that backseat on the southbound Hollywood Freeway as I found out for myself where the music is.

These three plays are sound paintings that move through the worlds of our grandparents (and their grandparents), channeled from deep sessions of listening to Paul Robeson work songs, Sidney Bechet blues, *ranchera* songs of Jorge Negrete, and the pure guitar soul of the Reverend Gary Davis and

Lightnin Hopkins.

These plays grew from quixotic challenges I made myself to write towards the feelings the music inspired within me, the emotional experience packed with memory and history that unlocked my curiosity for things beyond the blush of my own skin. Reading the plays of William Saroyan and Luis Valdez, not to mention the August Wilson of "*Joe Turner's Come and Gone*," only put red to the bull.

The helix of my plays spirals around a population of marginal Americans, those avoiding or ignored by census, working for the futures of their progeny (us), finding joy and pain in each other's company, and listening, for pleasure and for their spirit, to the music of their lives going by. The excruciating beauty of these sounds -- elevated to the stage, outside time and space -- is my subject. To really listen demands that you take into account your own helical relations to this country, its history of slavery, injustice and omission, but also its moments of exquisite freedom.

The music is where you feel it. I feel it in these plays.

Oliver Mayer

Los Angeles, CA

September 2007

JOE LOUIS BLUES

CHARACTERS:

Leila Rivers, a young black woman from Brooklyn
Demas Dean, "The Cornet King," a young black man from Long
Island
Sidney Bechet, sax master, an older black man from New Orleans
Vantyle Mayfield, a middle-aged black man from St. Croix
Joe Louis, the Heavyweight Champion of the World, a young
black man from the South
Barney, owner of the Mocha Club, an older Jewish man from
Brooklyn
Isaac, a piano accompanist, a younger Jewish man from Brooklyn
Announcer, the Voice of America, a young white man

PLACE:

The Blackbird Club, Harlem
The Hotel Theresa, Harlem
The Southern Tailor Shop, Harlem
Pompton Lakes, New Jersey
The world of the Radio

JOE LOUIS BLUES was developed at Columbia University, and
in a workshop production at the Los Angeles Theatre Center,
directed by Abdul Salaam El Razzac. It received its world
premiere at Thick Description, San Francisco in the year 2000,
directed by Tony Kelly. It received subsequent productions at the
Tiffany Theatres, Los Angeles, directed by L. Kenneth
Richardson; and at the Jomandi Theater, Atlanta, directed by
Buddy Butler.

ACT ONE

Scene 1

The BLACKBIRD CLUB, 143rd and Saint Nicholas Avenue,
January 9, 1942.

In the semi-dark, through a scrim, we see SIDNEY BECHET and
his New Orleans Feetwarmers. We hear Bechet's recording of
"BLUE HORIZON", the fat sax cadenzas and the joy of the blues.
Beside him DEMAS DEAN accompanies on cornet, looking cool
and sounding better. To the side, somewhat superfluous to the
band, LEILA RIVERS "leads" the band. She holds a baton and
waves it in rhythm, but she is beyond all doubts a prop, if a
beautiful one.

As the tune approaches the break, LEILA leaves off the baton
waving. The music is taking her somewhere, someplace joyous. She
opens her mouth to sing when --

VANTYLE MAYFIELD appears at the beaded doorway to the back
room of the club. They lock eyes. With a single gesture -- a throat-
cut -- he silences her.

The music continues past the break. They certainly don't need her,
but both Demas and Sidney register the loss of her voice in the
song. If anything it adds to the blues.

As she joylessly finds the rhythm with her baton, --

Scene 2

The MUSIC changes to something played double-time.

The scene shifts to the back room. Nothing fancy -- Coca Cola
crates, telephone, a radio.

Outside the beads, HOUSE enters. Takes a barstool, settles into
his office. No one bothers him.

Inside the beads, Vantyle is fiddling with the radio. All he's getting
is static. Leila pushes the beads aside.

LEILA: They wanna know is it time yet.

VAN: *(West Indian)* Who said they could listen? They got a club to play for!

LEILA: Nobody out there, Van.

VAN: Dickty niggers. Dog-assed dickty --

LEILA: Pot calls the kettle black.

VAN: No, woman. I'm no Southern Black -- it's another tribe. If they weren't so stupid you'd feel sorry for them.

LEILA: *(to herself)* Monkeychaser.

She brushes past him to the radio.

VAN: Busted. Nothing but static. Everything turns to crap, --

She finds the station. As she does, --

SPOT on ANNOUNCER. Tuxedoed and pommaded, ringside.

ANNOUNCER: Fifteen rounds or less for the Heavyweight Championship of the World!

Leila turns the sound down. As she does, the spot bumps to half while the ANNOUNCER continues -- we just can't hear him. Leila brushes past Van. He stops her.

VAN: You'd be all right if you had a sense of humor.

LEILA: So would you. Except for the bug up your butt.

VAN: Take one to know one.

Van puts a hand on her shoulder. It will wend its way down to her rear end. He grins -- she glares.

LEILA: You ain't gonna know mine noways.

VAN: Nice. You got to put out sometime... Li'l Leila....

LEILA: Maybe,....

Leila strokes Van's face, her hand wending its way down to his privates. Van responds.

LEILA: Maybe I will...if that's what it takes....

Then clamps down hard on his organ. Van writhes.

LEILA: But not with you. Get me?

VAN: Yeah.

LEILA: Yeah?

VAN: Yeah!

LEILA: Yeah.

Leila lets him go.

LEILA: Don't even try to run that shit on me. I been getting that since I was thirteen.

VAN: *(in discomfort)* I ought to put you out in the street!

LEILA: I been there before.

VAN: You don't seem to realize. I could be of some assistance.

LEILA: For what? To scratch my ass? I'll look you up next time it starts itching.

VAN: You won't get there alone, woman. *(they stare at each other)* You makes your breaks.

From outside, the MUSIC ends fast and without fanfare. Demas Dean enters on the run, cornet in hand.

DEMAS: Is it time?!! By God, we didn't miss it, did we?!!

VAN: Well if it ain't the Cornet King,....

Sidney Bechet enters, carrying his sax like a baby.

VAN: And *Le Plus Grand Monsieur* Bechet....

SIDNEY: *A votre service*, Boss.

DEMAS: Gimme some sugar, Peaches! *(grabs Leila, snuggles)* I need something to grab hold of.

LEILA: Latch on.

Demas squeezes her, then lets go. Van stares at them.

DEMAS: So where is he?

VAN: Who?

DEMAS: Who? Joe Louis Barrow, The Brown Bomber, The Dark Destroyer, The Whupper of Whitemen, six-two, two hundred pounds, forty-some wins mostly of the knockout variety, and the world's undisputed Champeen -- that's who! I'm talking about his highest and mightiest, --

VAN: Shut him up somebody!

Leila kisses Demas.

DEMAS: Jeez. That was more than delicious.

LEILA: *(as VAN watches her)* There's more where that come from.

SIDNEY: Youngfella nearly blew my wig, took everything double-time, afraid he'd miss King Joe.

DEMAS: I'm no different than any other red-blooded black American. Hey Vantyle, got yerself an empty club out there!

VAN: Joe Louis sure can mess with a man's business.

SIDNEY: Folks'll be here. To celebrate, or drown their sorrows. Or both.

DEMAS: I told you, Van. Nobody gonna be out this time of night. This a fight night, this a Joe Louis night. I told you that.

VAN: How can a coupla palookas drub each other for one tin dime?

DEMAS: Joe don't take drubbings. He gives 'em. And he got more tin dimes than a man can dream.

Demas slaps Sidney five on the blackhand side.

VAN: Barbaric excuse for a sport. Poor pat'etic fools, --

DEMAS: Don't mouth off about what you don't understand. See, when Joe fights, it's like churchgoing. Folks listen to get saved. Help me out, Bash.

SIDNEY: Joe ain't heavyweight. More like holyweight.

DEMAS: He' the King of them all!!

VAN: *(scoffing, to LEILA)* Another tribe.

DEMAS: Turn that sound up, Peaches. This fight's started!!

As she does, Announcer's spot bumps up. BELL sounds.

ANNOUNCER: --Joe Louis with his title on the line against Buddy Baer and here we go! -- They meet head-on in ring center -- Joe ducks a wild right -- fires a piston-like jab -- Baer to the body -- he's certainly come to fight --

Demas and Sidney lean close to the radio. Van, despite himself, can't help getting caught up in the drama. House listens from the bar. Only Leila stands apart unmoved.

ANNOUNCER: Baer weighed in at an even two-hundred-forty-one pounds of man-muscle and he towers over Joe with a full three-inch height advantage -- Boy he's some hunka man --

VAN: White boy too big for him.

DEMAS: So was Primo Carnera.

SIDNEY: Joe beat him like a redheaded stepchild.

Demas raises his fist as if he were Joe.

ANNOUNCER: OH!! -- There it is, Joe with a right cross to Buddy's handsome jaw --!!

DEMAS: Come on! Do it Joe --!!

ANNOUNCER: -- The Champ follows up to the midsection --

DEMAS: Come on now! Lick that dog --!!

VAN: Do this geechee ever stop gabbing?!!

ANNOUNCER: -- The Brown Bomber looking to end it now --
Baer gamely hanging in there, but it's not looking so good for him
and his fans -- swinging wildly now -- leaps in -- OH!!! -- right
haymaker! -- LOUIS IS STUNNED!!!!

Groaning and disbelief, even from Leila.

ANNOUNCER: The crowd on its feet -- History in the making --
Can Baer do it? -- Can he bring back the heavyweight title?

DEMAS: Bring back? To who?

ANNOUNCER: Can he do it? He keeps punching -- a real display
of the American fighting spirit --!!

DEMAS: Joe's American too!

ANNOUNCER: A barrage of wide blows -- Buddy going for broke
-- Louis crouching --

DEMAS: Stand up!

ANNOUNCER: -- Crouching --

DEMAS: Stand up to him --!!

VAN: You call that a king?

ANNOUNCER: OH!!! -- THUNDEROUS left hook!!

DEMAS: *(jumping up)* Which one?!! Which one?!!

ANNOUNCER: *(a touch of disappointment)* Louis really caught
him there, -- hooks again -- now to the body -- Buddy sagging on
the ropes -- wicked left to the ribs -- left to the jaw -- now the right
-- He's down!! The Challenger's down.

Much rejoicing.

ANNOUNCER: He'll never make the count. It's a kayo in Round
One.

Van turns the radio down.

DEMAS: My goodness yes. This is definitely a Joe Louis night.

SIDNEY: Had me a little scared when the big boy popped him.

DEMAS: Aw he just wanna give the people a good show -- din't worry me a bit!

SIDNEY: Almost gave you a heart-attack --

DEMAS: Well it all came out all right. Gotta hand it to that Brown Bomber. Sure can lay a white man flat. *(to VAN)* What'd I tell ya, Bossman? Ain't the best thing for blackfolk since black-eyed peas?

VAN: *(scoffing)* He all right.

DEMAS: All right?!!

VAN: For a backwoods boy.

DEMAS: Who you calling backwoods?

VAN: Southern dog-ass Negroes.

DEMAS: What? You ain't a Negro? Or you ain't a dog?

VAN: I ain't Southern.

DEMAS: Yeah, you from some little grass-skirt island!

VAN: Saint Croix a civilized island.

LEILA: Then how come you ain't?

DEMAS: Don't be talking down the South, man, 'cause lemme tell you something -- Saint Croix's a damn sight further south than Carolina!

VAN: But it ain't backwoods.

DEMAS: What's wrong with backwoods?

VAN: Backwoods full of unlearned geechees.

DEMAS: Geechees, huh? Well let this geechee show you --!

LEILA: It ain't worth it, Demas.

DEMAS: But you heard him, --

LEILA: I'm trying not to.

SIDNEY: Demas, we gotta woik together.

DEMAS: I know. *(grins at VAN)* Unlearned, huh? Somebody sure learned Joe how to punch.

VAN: Let's see can he put two sentences together.

DEMAS: Turn up the damn radio.

VAN: *(refusing to move)* He your king, not mine.

Demas brushes past him to turn up the radio.

Spot up on Announcer with JOE LOUIS, handsome in a velvet robe, towel over his head. In his hand, of all things, is an apple. He will eat it before and after the interview, but not during. His voice is low and gentle.

ANNOUNCER: Congratulations Champ.

JOE: Thanks.

ANNOUNCER: Some knockout.

JOE: He a strong man....Just glad I got there first.

ANNOUNCER: A whole lot of your colored fans are mighty glad too.

DEMAS: You hep to that!

ANNOUNCER: So what's next, Joe?

DEMAS: MISTER Louis to you.

JOE: Don' know.

ANNOUNCER: Well, uh, who's the next opponent?

JOE: Don' know.

ANNOUNCER: Um....

DEMAS: Ask him a real question, fool!

VAN: *(scoffing)* "Don' know"....

ANNOUNCER: Bet you're going up to Harlem to celebrate?

JOE: Yeah. Good people up there.

ANNOUNCER: Why sure, --

To Announcer's surprise, Joe takes the mike.

JOE: I just wanna thank all the people out there listening and pulling for me. Every little bit helps. Thanks.

Demas beams.

ANNOUNCER: *(takes the mike back)* That's uh swell champ. You're a real credit to your race.

DEMAS: Our race put your race on its ass.

ANNOUNCER: And Uncle Sam can certainly use those muscles of yours to kayo Hitler and the Nips.

VAN: DAMN Uncle Sam!

DEMAS: Say what?

VAN: You heard me.

ANNOUNCER: *(turning away from JOE)* In the midst of our great struggle for world freedom, boxers everywhere are flocking to the Armed Services to defend America's title. The proceeds for tonight's fight, including Joe Louis's entire fight purse, will be donated to the Army Relief Fund. Thanks, Joe, for doing your duty, --

Van flicks the radio off. Announcer and Joe vanish.

DEMAS: What'd you do that for?

VAN: Joe Louis just another fool give good money away.

DEMAS: Fool? Who you calling fool?

SIDNEY: Bossman, there's a war on, --

VAN: Yeah, we losing.

DEMAS: 'Cause of people like you we're losing. What kind of American are you?

VAN: You gonna fight this war, Dean?

DEMAS: I'm working.

VAN: Scared?

DEMAS: Hell no.

VAN: You gonna join up?

DEMAS: I'm a busy man --

VAN: They gonna draft your ass soon enough. Then whatchu gonna do?

DEMAS: Then...I'll go...if I gotta.

VAN: Then you a fool!

DEMAS: *(under his breath)* And you a Communist.

Van rises, steps to. Sidney steps in between.

VAN: You say something?

SIDNEY: Demas just saying how glad he is that Joe coming home to Harlem.

DEMAS: Yeah that's it. *(grins)* King Joe in Little Africa! Natives gonna do some stomping! You know people wanna dance when Joe do his thing. Them big clubs be hopping. Say Peaches, how 'bout you and me head on over and join the fun?

LEILA: Swell.

VAN: You got a gig to play. After hours you can go find your damn king. But now you get to work. I ain't pay you to please yourself.

The others rise.

DEMAS: Yassuh! Sho nuff, Massah!

SIDNEY: Gotta hand it to ya, Boss -- bizness foist.

Sidney motions for smokes. Van gives Sidney a matchbox.

DEMAS: *(snuggling)* Got something to tell ya, Peaches. *(to VAN)* You not so evil as you sound, you ol' buzzard. I saw you smile when Joe landed that left hook. I'm on to you, brother. *(about to exit)* Enjoy the show. I'ma set the stand on fire.

VAN: Glad you remind me. Lighten up on the solos. The people pay to hear Bechet.

Demas exits muttering. As he passes House, he is careful to look down and away. Leila starts to exit as well. Van blocks the way.

LEILA: I got a gig to play.

VAN: They can start wit'out you.

Leila shrugs. Sits.

LEILA: Why you hate this war? Scared?

VAN: Not fear. Agitation. Stupid t'ings agitate me. People rushing into foolishness. If they'd only stop to t'ink --

LEILA: Now you're a thinker.

VAN: I am my own man.

LEILA: Sounds lonely.

MUSIC begins, mellow. Bechet takes the lead.

VAN: This my club. Nothing fancy, no battle of the bands, no chorus line, no kitchen. But we got Sidney Bechet twice a week. Used to be the big man. Now he don't cost so much, but he like it here and the people come. Why not? Drinks is cheap, music good, and we got Li'l Leila leading the band. You like leading the band?

LEILA: You mean do I like to shake my rear for a buncha drunks and number runners? I'm a singer.

VAN: You can't sing.

LEILA: I damn well can.

VAN: You ain't no Et'el Waters.

LEILA: You never gimme the chance you bastid!

VAN: Easy woman. I don't give you nothing. Not till you show me what kind of woman you are.

LEILA: You ain't gonna give up till I take off my shirt.

VAN: That don't interest me.

LEILA: Like hell.

VAN: I giving you some advice.

LEILA: Thanks Professor, but I'm doing fine.

VAN: You could do better. *(beat)* Don't settle. You end up with nothing.

LEILA: What's it to ya?

VAN: Nothing. So get out there.

She exits. Van does figures on scrap paper.

Scene 3

As MUSIC plays on, --

A NUMBER RUNNER approaches House. Gives him a paper bag. Splits. House examines the contents without flash. Sidney ducks through the beads, finds his stash in the sax case. Beams, rolls himself a monster cigar-sized splif known as a mezz-roll, and takes an experienced hit.Demas enters. House watches him.

SIDNEY: Boy.

DEMAS: Say Bash.

House continues to bird-dog him.

SIDNEY: Don't pay him no mind, Son. House don't got nothing for you.

DEMAS: I ain't got nothing for House. Numbers ain't my thing. Weed neither.

House splits.

SIDNEY: *(tokes)* Better get back on the stand 'for the Boss gets sore.

DEMAS: Let him. I'm so juiced on Joe Louis my soul wanna come out and dance! That righteous right hook of his! Man! I wish I had one of those!

SIDNEY: Let Joe do the fighting, boy.

DEMAS: And I'll do the celebrating.

SIDNEY: Now you cooking Creole.

DEMAS: Everytime I see him in the papers or the newsreels...it's like...it's like I'm him.

Demas shadow-boxes lustily -- he's no boxer.

SIDNEY: You wouldn't like getting hit back.

DEMAS: Man, sometimes I start seeing myself, bigger than life, putting it to some poor sucker. And the fella I'm beating on starts looking more and more like Vantyle!

Van looks up but stays silent.

SIDNEY: Careful now.

DEMAS: I swear that island monkeychaser has it in for us. Geechee. I shoulda kicked some sense in that skull of his. Don't he give a damn about us?

SIDNEY: Keep it down, boy --

DEMAS: And the way he's always leering at Leila, like she's something good to eat or something. You know he better stop that. I can't feature that. Don't he know the little gal and me is getting married?

Van reacts, quietly.

SIDNEY: Say what?

DEMAS: We getting out of this hole. I got plans. I'm gonna take her on out to California.

SIDNEY: Is that right.

DEMAS: Oh I got plans.

SIDNEY: But ain't Leila wanna stay here?

DEMAS: Yeeeah, but she'll change her mind.

SIDNEY: What make you so sure?

DEMAS: All in the plan.

SIDNEY: Take two to plan two. Listen to the woman. Hear what she got to say. Otherwise them plans ain't gonna mean too much. *(beat)* You really getting hitched?

DEMAS: I'm gonna hit her with it tonight.

Van reacts again, agitated.

SIDNEY: She don't know yet?

DEMAS: But she loves me.

SIDNEY: *(shrugs)* Well God bless you then.

DEMAS: This is my night...!

The heretofore unknown backdoor opens from the alley. JOE LOUIS enters, his silhouette taking up the entire doorway. Immaculate except for an abrasion under one eye.

Van jumps up, Sidney backs up. Demas freezes.

JOE: Pardon me. Mind if I duck in here?

VAN: Go ahead. We got a front entrance --

JOE: People get a little...excited.

VAN: Of course. Mister Louis, isn't it?

JOE: Call me Joe. I asked the driver did he know someplace small. I don't feel like swinging. I'm happy listening to a little blues and maybe having a little down-home Southern cooking.

VAN: We don't have a kitchen. B-But I'll see if I can muster something, --

JOE: No no. That's all right.

They all stand awkwardly. Then Van jumps forward.

VAN: Come in. Come in. This a hot little club. Hottest club this side of Hades. Get you a fine table near the band --

JOE: Fine in here.

VAN: Whatever you say. *(brushes off a crate)* Anyt'ing for King Joe.

JOE: I'm no king. But thanks.

VAN: *(hissing, to SIDNEY)* Pick it up, eh?

Sidney starts off.

JOE: You Bechet?

SIDNEY: That's me.

JOE: *(shakes hands)* Pleasure.

SIDNEY: What do you like, son? It'd be my pleasure to play it.

JOE: Play me a blues.

SIDNEY: *C'est bon.* You got yerself a blues. *(to DEMAS as he goes)* C'mon Dean, let's show him something.

DEMAS: *(still frozen)* You go. I'll be there.

Sidney exits.

VAN: How 'bout a drink?

JOE: No thanks.

Joe looks through the beads at the bandstand. MUSIC begins, a Bechet blues classic. Joe watches, then nods.

JOE: Got yourself a nice conductor.

VAN: Her? You like her? *(JOE shrugs, smiles)* Okay. Everything can be arranged.

Van exits quickly. Joe and Demas are alone. Demas stares, Joe seems shy, almost afraid to look Demas in the eye. Demas wants to say something but nothing comes out. Then Van returns with Leila. They are fighting in whispers.

VAN: Entertain the man!

LEILA: What the hell --!

VAN: Don't be stupid! Now's yer chance!

Van pushes her in front of Joe.

VAN: *(honeyed)* This is Leila. Our lead singer and star-to-be.

Joe smiles at Leila. She does not seem overwhelmed. Van backs up, smiling. Demas grabs him as he passes by.

DEMAS: How come you bring Peaches --?

VAN: You gonna step in her way? Hey, you can still get hitched, ...After.

DEMAS: Don't bring me down, man.

VAN: You down for the count.

Van exits. Demas hovers, straining to hear.

LEILA: Looking for somebody?

JOE: Found her.

LEILA: Congratulations.

JOE: You the prettiest singer I ever saw.

LEILA: That's why I'm so famous. Why you here? Harlem must be going wild.

JOE: I don't feel like going wild. Not yet, anyway.

LEILA: Aintcha gonna celebrate?

JOE: I sure hope so.

LEILA: Do you want me to get you something?

JOE: I want you to come out with me.

LEILA: When?

JOE: Tonight.

LEILA: I'm working.

JOE: We don't gotta go right yet. Why don't you go sing?

LEILA: I don't think so, Champ.

JOE: Sing me something.

LEILA: I'm not a singer. Not here. They're just showing me off, Joe. Don't care what the hell I sound like. Customers come to see the *cafe au lait*.

JOE: Hey, everybody likes chocolate....

LEILA: Not me. I don't eat nothing darker than me.

JOE: Yeah, I guess.

LEILA: *(finally smiles)* This is pretty crazy.

JOE: But good. Don't get much of this. Training all the time. Don't get out so much as I'd like.

LEILA: I don't believe it.

JOE: Well maybe a bit,....

LEILA: How's your eye?

JOE: I might just need me a nurse,....

Demas involuntarily steps in the way.

DEMAS: Uh, excuse me, uh, I don't wanna, uh --

JOE: Joe Louis.

DEMAS: I know.

LEILA: What.

DEMAS: Maybe we oughta go. Thought you'd wanna do your stuff, you know, for Joe. Bash and me'll play, you sing.

JOE: You sing blues?

LEILA: Cheap swing. Movie tunes.

JOE: Sing me some blues.

DEMAS: Yeah, go on. *(she demurs)* What.

JOE: What is it?

LEILA: Nothing, I just don't want to.

DEMAS: Bash and me'll help --

LEILA: I SAID NO.

Awkward pause.

DEMAS: She's fine -- I-I mean a fine singer. Sings them radio tunes better than on the Hit Parade. Peaches, she --

JOE: Peaches?

DEMAS: Yeah, she's my g--

LEILA: Do you got something to do?

DEMAS: Same thing you gotta do.

LEILA: I'm sitting this one out.

DEMAS: She's really something. All she needs is a break. Of course, there's breaks and there's breaks. See me, I'd just as soon take her out to California and have a mess of little brown babies like their mama, --

LEILA: DEMAS!!

DEMAS: Like I said. *(a wave of awe towards JOE)* Jeez. I can't tell you what it's like, standing here next to you. It's...it's a dream. I was just listening to the radio, --

JOE: Thanks. *(putting on his coat)* Miss Leila leaving now.

LEILA: What?

JOE: You ain't singing. Why stay? *(takes her arm)* It'll be all right. Come on. I got a car waiting, --

Leila resists. To everyone's surprise, Demas intervenes.

DEMAS: Do as the man says. *(LEILA stares hard at him)* You go on. We'll be all right.

LEILA: What are you doing?

DEMAS: It'll be all right.

(beat)

LEILA: All right.

JOE: Get your coat. It's cold out there --

LEILA: It's over th--

DEMAS: I got it.

Demas gets it, starts to put it on Leila. Joe takes over. Puts it over Leila's shoulders. Demas in a daze.

JOE: Thanks.

DEMAS: You two have yourselves a great time. *(as they exit)* And Mister Louis?

JOE: Yeah?

DEMAS: I'll never forget this.

They exit. Demas stands there. Van peers at him through the beads. The MUSIC grows sexier and more lowdown. Demas brings both hands over his mouth.

Scene 4

Spot up on Announcer.

ANNOUNCER: It's official. The War Department has just announced that Joe Louis, who just donated fifty thousand dollars to Navy Relief, will not only place his title on the line against Big Abe Simon next month, but will contribute his ENTIRE paycheck to Army Relief. Here's to you, Joe. You are America's champ, and a credit to your race. And now, back to Your Hit Parade,....

Spot off. Radio music as lights rise slow on Joe and Leila making love. Clothes strewn about.

LEILA: Stop that.

JOE: Ain't doing nothing.

LEILA: You're making me crazy.

JOE: Good.

She pulls away, he pulls her back.

JOE: Where you going?

LEILA: I'm here. *(kisses him)* Sweet Joe.

JOE: You sweet.

LEILA: No I'm not.

JOE: Looks sweet...tastes sweet....

LEILA: Don't let it fool ya.

JOE: How come I'm sweet?

LEILA: Your eyes. You got a little boy's eyes.

JOE: I'm a man.

LEILA: Not your eyes. *(beat)* How you knock somebody out?

JOE: Skill.

LEILA: It's more than that. You must be so mad in there, --

JOE: You can't fight mad.

LEILA: That's the only way.

JOE: You like fighting!

LEILA: Hell, I didn't even like you till tonight.

JOE: Ol' Buddy Baer tagged me pretty good tonight, --

LEILA: *(touches his eye)* You mean here?

JOE: Naw. Down here. *(his ribs)* I'd rather take ten shots to the head than one good kidney punch.

LEILA: Hurt?

JOE: Only when I breathe.

LEILA: *(suggestively)* Didn't seem to bother you none.

JOE: I'm an old pro. *(snuggles)* You could do something for me.

LEILA: What do you have in mind?

JOE: Sing me something.

LEILA: Why?

JOE: Puts me at ease. Go on. Sing the blues. *(she pulls away)*

What's up, Girl?

LEILA: Nothing's up, I just don't want to.

JOE: *(reaching out for her)* Don't worry about it, baby --

LEILA: *(swats his hand away)* Don't baby me, man!

JOE: So you don't sing.

LEILA: Not the blues.

JOE: What's wrong with the blues?

LEILA: Nothing....Just something lowdown about the man done leave me....Sounds good to ya, don't it?

JOE: What you mad about?

LEILA: You ever see how blues singers always got a smile on? One of them no-gut flabby I-forgive-ya smiles. Forgiving the sonofabitch she's singing about, the muthafucka who fucked her, then left her without a dime.

JOE: That's the blues.

LEILA: That's what I despise. Every time I sing the blues I can feel it, and I think, you liver-lipped witch, how dare you smile? What kinda woman are you anyway? But every night, the men gotta ask me to sing the blues. Especially the Southerners.

JOE: They a long way from home. *(beat)* Blues don't always gotta be like that.

LEILA: I don't like pain.

JOE: Sometimes the hurt's good. *(beat)* Blues the kinda thing you hear on the porch when you down South. You got a Co' Cola in your hand, you got your people with you,....You're home. One of the old folk'll start humming, drumming a beat on the steps, maybe somebody else got a mouth organ, a guitar. Most of all you got your voice and your hands. You put it all together, pretty soon you got something cooking. Nobody got to go to school for that. Nobody got to be scared. We all been there...or will be soon. The old folk know 'cause they seen the real pain. But instead of getting mad they smiling. Making some damn good music too.

LEILA: It's not worth it.

JOE: Them feelings, they come out one way or the other.

LEILA: I can't afford it, Joe. I can't let that stuff out. If I didn't feel so damn angry, I wouldn't know who I was. So I'll be damned if I give that away, just 'cause some man asked me to sing the blues. *(beat)* See, I gotta look out for myself.

JOE: Who your man?

LEILA: Don't usually give myself away so easy.

JOE: How 'bout that cat with the trumpet?

LEILA: What kinda man loves the fights more than a full-grown woman?

JOE: Not me.

LEILA: He's just a man.

JOE: Then what am I?

LEILA: I don't know yet.

JOE: Well I'm a man too.

"WHY DON'T YOU DO RIGHT?" by Peggy Lee on the radio.

LEILA: Hear that?

JOE: It's good.

LEILA: That's a white girl. What the hell does she know?

JOE: She know how to sing that song.

Before she can retort, he kisses her. For a moment, they make love. Leila seems deep in thought. Joe lets her go.

JOE: So what do you want, Girl?

LEILA: A break I guess. Not too much really, just uh...movies, radio, record gigs...stuff like that. *(beat)* I wanna sing.

JOE: But not the blues.

LEILA: I could learn.

(beat)

JOE: I'll see what I can do.

LEILA: I don't need any kinda jive, --

JOE: No jive. I know some people. The guy at the Mocha Club. I'll talk to him.

LEILA: The Mocha Club? They're on the radio all the time, --

JOE: Hey. It's the least I can do. Now gimme some sugar.

She gets on top of him.

LEILA: I just want you to know, I didn't come here for any favors.

JOE: No favors.

LEILA: *(can't help smiling)* Jeez....Nobody ever gave a damn....

JOE: Fine woman like you....

LEILA: Oh they give a damn about that. But nobody ever gave me something just to give it. *(beat)* So what is it that you want?

JOE: I got what I want right here in my own two hands.

LEILA: Oh baby --! *(lays a big kiss on him)* You're bigger than life! I can't believe I'm so lucky, that you're free, that you don't got a wife somewheres, --

JOE: I do. But don't worry about it.

Leila stops. Then jumps up looking for her clothes.

LEILA: Goddammit.

JOE: What's the matter?

LEILA: Thanks for the ride.

JOE: Don't do that.

LEILA: I don't do this kinda thing, Joe.

JOE: Don't get mad, --

LEILA: Mad? I don't care who the FUCK you are. I shoulda known you'd pull the same goddamn --

JOE: I'm sorry.

LEILA: I thought -- *(stops)* I thought you were better.

JOE: I don't wanna hurt you. I don't wanna hurt nobody. Don't wanna be sorry for nothing I ever done.

LEILA: So what?

JOE: So don't go.

LEILA: I don't take handouts.

JOE: No handouts.

LEILA: Then what? Outa the kindness of your heart? Spare me.

JOE: You a beautiful woman. And you don't got a man.

LEILA: That's the truth.

JOE: Be my friend. Stick with me. I give you what you need. I swear to that.

LEILA: And what do I do for you?

JOE: Stick with me.

A business-like pause.

LEILA: All right.

JOE: Well that's all right.

LEILA: What I want? *(her demands)* I want to sing at the Mocha Club.

JOE: You got it.

LEILA: I'm through uptown. I wanna live down.

JOE: I'll get you a room.

LEILA: I want a doorman.

JOE: You a golddigger. *(off her evil look)* I didn't mean it, Girl. I'll see what I can do.

Joe brings her back to bed.

LEILA: You as good as your word?

JOE: I'm better than that.

LEILA: Why you give all your money away?

JOE: I got more.

LEILA: What if you run out?

JOE: Just money. I love my country.

LEILA: Shit. Sure ain't no businessman. *(beat)* You really don't mind my mouth?

JOE: It's pretty.

LEILA: I mean what comes out of it.

JOE: If I gets mad, you'll be the first to know.

LEILA: Joe?

JOE: Yeah.

LEILA: I wanna sing.

JOE: Then sing.

They make love.

Scene 5

"WHAT IS THIS THING CALLED LOVE?" by Bechet plays.
Van approaches House, who removes a roll of bills and peels off
several into Van's hand. Van pours House a drink. They kibbitz,
Van animatedly.

Backroom, Demas sits sulking and drinking. MUSIC ends. Sidney
enters.

SIDNEY: Get up, Boy.

DEMAS: Naw man.

SIDNEY: You going to hell in a handbasket.

DEMAS: I'm cool.

SIDNEY: This ain't cool. Quit it. What's done is done and they did
it. Better raise yourself. Bossman be watching you.

DEMAS: *(drinks)* Let him. Island bastid.

SIDNEY: Keep it down!

DEMAS: Two-bit mammy-jamming monkeychasing --

SIDNEY: He's right behind ya!

DEMAS: Think I care? I'll tell him to his face --!!

Sidney grabs Demas hard. Pins him to the wall.

SIDNEY: Listen. You blow your wig, you lose this gig, and gigs is
hard to come by. Draft Board gonna scoop you up. I don't want to
start writing postcards to no Private Dean in charge of latrines,
much less on the front. In combat? Kid, you'd never make it.
(lets him go) Let's go, Dean. I'll take you home. *(DEMAS starts to
cry)* Boy, what are you doing?

DEMAS: I'm no good alone, Bash.

SIDNEY: Hell, I'm here, ain't I?

DEMAS: Not quite what I had in mind.

SIDNEY: You takes what you gets, Boy. And you don't never give away your best stash.

DEMAS: Now you tell me! *(growing animated)* Damn! Any other man, Bash, any other man I'd -- I'd cut him for even looking at her --!

SIDNEY: Would you now?

DEMAS: Well maybe not cut him but *(makes a fist)* One of these right in the kisser. Like my man Joe -- *(winces)* Like Joe. But I didn't give nothing away. And even if I did, --*(grins)* It was Joe Louis Barrow, in the flesh. Courteous, and well-spoken,...And big as a brick shithouse. I never seen so much man. Can't refuse a man like that. Can't refuse him nothing. How you supposed to refuse a king?

SIDNEY: I know how you is, Boy, but I'm sorry. Come a choice and you chose.

Sidney removes the half-smoked mezzroll and lights up.

SIDNEY: You need a job where you can woik the daytime, a man's hours. Tire yourself out, get her off your mind. Save up a little silver while you're at it.

DEMAS: Naw.

SIDNEY: What? You afraid of woik?

DEMAS: It's just -- The Draft. *(confidential)* See Bash, if I'm single and I'm working days, you know I'm a sitting duck. That's why I thought if Leila wanted to...I mean, I love her too....

SIDNEY: So that's why you was itching to get hitched.

DEMAS: I just don't wanna have to -- I don't wanna fight.

Sidney smokes deep.

SIDNEY: I may just have something to save your butt. Now listen. Uncle Sidney got himself full half-ownership of the Southern Tailor Shop down on 129th and Saint Nick. I's a man of means.

DEMAS: You? A tailor?

SIDNEY: Like to keep it unner my hat.

DEMAS: I can learn to tailor.

SIDNEY: Got an opening for a pants presser.

DEMAS: Brothers gotta have them zoot suits!

SIDNEY: But don't lose this gig neither. You ain't a half-bad tooter if you'd woik at it.

DEMAS: I don't got it no more.

SIDNEY: Well then get it! What kinda musicianeer are you anyway? Just 'cause you lost your sweet thang? That oughta make you wanna play better! You oughta know by now, Boy. No matter what happens, no matter how you feel. You tell it to the music, and the music tells it back to you. That's the life there is to a musicianeer. *(takes a hit)* What do you say, King?

DEMAS: Messes with my lungs.

SIDNEY: I'm talking about the music!

DEMAS: I don't know. Look at you. Toppest cat this side of Satchmo, and you playing a lowdown dirty hole like this.

SIDNEY: This hole make good music.

DEMAS: You could do better. Downtown.

SIDNEY: I played that. With the music it don't matter where, or what kind neither. What counts is you're making it.

DEMAS: White folks pay top dollar.

SIDNEY: I got what I need. *(another hit)* Times like these make a man wanna go *incognegro*.

DEMAS: Say what?

SIDNEY: You a free man.

DEMAS: I don't wanna be free. I want Leila.

SIDNEY: She'll be back.

DEMAS: She don't want me.

SIDNEY: Call her.

DEMAS: She don't got a phone.

SIDNEY: Naw! Wit' your horn!

DEMAS: Call her? Call her what?

SIDNEY: You youngsters, you just ain't in touch.

DEMAS: Man, I just play my horn. I don't think about it.

SIDNEY: Well start!! Didn't I ever tell you about Goola?

DEMAS: Goola?

SIDNEY: That was my sweet dog. Never a better.

DEMAS: And you called him.

SIDNEY: How'd you know? This was back in France, just after the Foist War. He loved the music. Real intelligent black-eyed Shepherd, part wolf. I used to let him run free through the streets of Lyon --

DEMAS: Lyon?

SIDNEY: That's France. I think he had him a little girlfriend and I can't say I blame him, France is a mighty fine place. Treat you good. About as close to home as I ever been,....

DEMAS: I thought this was home.

SIDNEY: Yeah but -- France is close to Africa. *(beat)* So I let the boy roam. But if I wanted him, if I really wanted that boy, well then i'd tilt my horn back and let out the biggest-assed riff I could muster, like I was Papa Bach or something. Veins be popping. And with every note I'd be saying *(half-sings)* WHERE'S GOOOOLA, WHERE'S THAT SWEET BOY? And damned if he wasn't scratching at the door.

DEMAS: Prob'ly was hungry.

SIDNEY: He came 'cause I called him. If you want her, call. Use what you got, don't hold nothing back.

DEMAS: *(almost plays, then)* I don't think I can just now.

SIDNEY: Tell you what. I'll send her a message for you. This won't do the trick, but at least it'll keep us on her mind.

DEMAS: What you gonna play?

SIDNEY: That song she like.

DEMAS: Sleepy Time? Talk about a dumb song.

SIDNEY: What counts is what you do wit' it.

Sidney about to exit. Gives Demas an avuncular pat.

SIDNEY: Just know who you are, man, who you are. And don't be thinking and drinking too much. Look what it do to the white folk.

Sidney exits. Demas fingers the cornet.

DEMAS: *(to himself)* Come on back.

Van grins goodbye to House. Enters. His smile fades.

VAN: Dean. Why you ain't play? I ain't pay you to lay there.

DEMAS: Then don't pay me.

VAN: Say again.

DEMAS: I quit. I'm sick of it.

VAN: What?

DEMAS: I got plans, I ain't wasting no more time in no lowdown sloppy jetblack dive, I got places to go --!

VAN: Who's stopping you?

DEMAS: Can't get there from here, m'dear.

VAN: There the door.

DEMAS: You gonna be sorry.

VAN: What I got to be sorry about?

DEMAS: You busted up me and Leila!!

VAN: I just give her the chance.

DEMAS: Someone's got to do a lot to me. But I can get plenty mean, Van.

VAN: Don't t'reaten me. All I want is you go back to work. Or if you leaving, leave. Choose. I can get a new trumpet anytime.

DEMAS: CORNET!! You never did give a damn about any of us.

VAN: What the HELL you crying about Leila?! I t'ought you was tougher than that.

DEMAS: But I lo-- *(can't seem to say the word)*

VAN: You don't even know the woman. Cold, Dean. She don't let no man close. She too good for the likes of you and me. We stones in the river, she go dancing on top of our heads. You dreaming the love part.

DEMAS: What we had was a dream, --

VAN: QUIT THAT JIVE!

DEMAS: WHY CAN'T I KEEP DREAMING?!!

VAN: I hired a body, a can to swing. Sex, not love. Try to minimize that romantic jive. Now everybody ga-ga, like she DEEP or somet'ing. There is nothing to love.

DEMAS: Deep enough for Joe.

VAN: Ain't saying much.

DEMAS: You really wanna tangle.

VAN: Worship your king in the ring. 'Cause out of it he's just another customer. *(DEAN about to drink)* And quit drinking my liquor!!

DEMAS: I'm paying!!

Demas flings the contents of his pocket on the table. Coins, handkerchief, whatever.

VAN: Hell Dean! You living like you need permission from some woman! Joe Louis done you a favor.

DEMAS: Get outa my face.

VAN: You the kind who always try to please, get along and smile real nice and don't make nobody mad. Meanwhile the witch kick yer teeth down yer t'roat. What kinda man are ya?

DEMAS: *(giving ground)* You gonna make me show you.

VAN: I already see it. You ain't a man at all. You some kinda lapdog. You what they call a sooner.

DEMAS: Don't say another word --!

VAN: Sooner bark than bite. Sooner run than fight.

Demas steps to, fist raised.

VAN: Go on. T'row one like King Joe do. Go on, Boy!!

Demas cocks the fist, body aquiver. Can't do it. He sits.

VAN: *(almost brotherly)* Man, when you gonna stand up for yerself?

DEMAS: I can't fight. Never hit a man in my life.

VAN: You sure like other folks scuffling.

DEMAS: I wish I could be like Joe. Then I'd kick your ass.

VAN: You could. You just afraid to try.

DEMAS: But I'm still a man!!

VAN: No Dean. In this world we got to prove it. Stop dreaming about Joe Louis. Scuff yer own knuckles.

DEMAS: You think I shoulda decked her?

VAN: NO!! I'm talking about a change. A real change.

DEMAS: You really are a Communist.

VAN: No I ain't a Communist. Guess I ought to be, I just love money too much. *(beat)* No Dean. I'm telling you. You can be a bigger man.

DEMAS: Like you? No thanks.

VAN: I can be a bigger man too. *(moves away)* You don't got to listen to me. I get tired of talking to meself. *(resumes doing figures)*

DEMAS: How come you always doing them figures?
VAN: I be gone soon anyhow. What counts is I escape.

DEMAS: Escape what?

VAN: Blackness.

DEMAS: Man that's you.

VAN: This place just makes me blacker. That's why I busting out.

DEMAS: With them figures?

VAN: Foolproof.

DEMAS: You trying to hit the numbers!

VAN: Ain't trying nothing. This scientific. *(motions DEAN close)* Ever play?

DEMAS: Coupla times.

VAN: Hit?

DEMAS: Naw. Only bet a penny anyway.

VAN: That's 'cause you ain't got a system. Only way to beat the racket. Stay with it. Double the bet every day --

DEMAS: Double it?

VAN: Every day. Take money to make money.

DEMAS: Gonna take a lotta money.

VAN: High stakes, big breaks.

DEMAS: If I was you I'd take that cash you been saving and invest in a nice little plot of California sunshine.

VAN: I buy me own island when this hit.

DEMAS: Thanks...for taking my mind off her.

VAN: Yeah...I'll admit...woman like that, unattached,.... Well a man can fall. But to fall is weakness. You must stand up. Take a lesson from Joe Louis. The choice is up to you.

DEMAS: *(nods)* I'm gonna take your advice.

VAN: Yeah?

DEMAS: I'm gonna conquer this fear insida me if it's the last thing I do. Stop settling for less. Demand respect.

VAN: *(nods)* That's right.

DEMAS: It just occurred to me. You're scared of something till you get there. But once you're there, hell. It ain't that scary anymore.

VAN: Amen!

DEMAS: I'm gonna join up. *(VAN stops, glares)* What?

VAN: Why do I waste my time...?!!

DEMAS: There's fellas losing their lives, Van! I'ma stand up and fight!!

VAN: So you can lose yours?

DEMAS: Don't you love this country?

VAN: What have I got to love? What have I GOT to love? Wake up Dean. Slave days over!

DEMAS: Watch it --!

VAN: You as dirt-black dumb as the rest of them dickty niggers. Fight 'cause they tell you to fight. Die 'cause they want you to die. That's the way this whole thing was planned, fool!!

DEMAS: I'm not as dumb as you think. I can see right through your ass. You the scared one. That's it, in't it? You're pissing in your pants!!

VAN: Of course I am. But I'll fight my fight. MY fight.

DEMAS: You'll hide. That's the trouble with blackfolk. They don't stand up --!

VAN: You talk like a cracker.

DEMAS: Well they ain't all wrong.

VAN: *(losing it)* Go on then! Go fight they war!

DEMAS: You done yet?

VAN: You white. White with fright. You'll never make the grade.

DEMAS: I QUIT!!!

Demas exits. Van's scrap papers are wet with liquor.

Scene 6

LEILA puts on a stylish dress, her best nylons with the seam down the back, and her Betty Grable pumps.

"SLEEPY TIME DOWN SOUTH" scratchily on the radio.

ANNOUNCER: Sidney Bechet and his New Orleans Feetwarmers, a song entitled "Sleepy Time Down South"....Certainly one of the most expressive Negro saxophonists in the popular repetoire,....

RADIO THEME MUSIC, Announcer alters his voice.

ANNOUNCER: And now the news. It's Private Joe Louis! The Champ took his mandatory physical this morning. Not surprisingly, the Army found him fit for service. Private Joe sets the example for America's sports celebrities -- heart and soul towards victory. Now it's a fight to the finish and we're mighty glad Joe's on our side. In a speech at Madison Square Garden last night, the Brown Bomber said that

Joe, in civvies, joins Announcer.

JOE: I have only done what any red-blood American would do. We'll do our part 'cause we're on God's side. Thank you.

As spot dims on them, --

Lights rise on the MOCHA CLUB, a white blues establishment run by BARNEY, a Brooklyn Jew. ISAAC, the accompanist, plays around on the piano.

BARNEY: Told ya she'd throw my whole day's schedule out the window!

ISAAC: Can't count on 'em, Boss.

BARNEY: Try to be nice, do a person a favor, look what happens.

ISAAC: You got a lunch date with the RCA Victor people in an hour.

BARNEY: I can't eat. I got a pain here.

ISAAC: Gas?

BARNEY: I wish it were. Get me a glass of milk, wouldya? *(ISAAC starts off)* Crazy, huh?

ISAAC: Absolutely.

BARNEY: Fifteen years ago I was in Dental School. Now look at me for chrissakes. Waiting around for schwartzes, --!

ISAAC: Yep.

BARNEY: All 'cause of them blues singers.

ISAAC: Sure been a lot of them.

BARNEY: I was thinking about the ladies.

ISAAC: So was I. You certainly seem to get along.

BARNEY: That's 'cause we do get along.

ISAAC: *(smiling wryly)* The darker the berry, --

BARNEY: Not like that. *(waxes philosophic)* Them colored girls, they're different. They're not like us. I seen the best of 'em, you can vouch for that. And even when they aren't the most attractive-looking creatures in the world, well, there's something there just as good as looks. Better, even. Women sing the blues best. Am I right? 'Cause when they sing, you start seeing and hearing 'em different. You start believing in 'em. And before you know what exactly hit you, they suddenly are the most beautiful women in the world.

ISAAC: You wanna sandwich?

BARNEY: Milk. Maybe half a sandwich.

ISAAC: Coming right up.

Isaac exits. The Leila enters, looking great.

BARNEY: Ah ha!

LEILA: You scared me!

BARNEY: You're late!

When Leila speaks it is with a slightly affected accent.

LEILA: The trains! Really are quite a pain. It'll be easier once I move downtown.

BARNEY: Listen, Miss --

LEILA: Harlem is another world. It had its day. But today's world is more -- how shall I say? -- Sophisticated.

BARNEY: I know women who would stand in the rain for a chance to audition here.

LEILA: *(stunned)* Audition?

BARNEY: Take your coat off.

LEILA: Thanks.

BARNEY: Let's get down to business. *(watches her)* Say. You're a beautiful woman. Not too many singers are. That's something in your favor. Wonderful. Stupendous. Joe Louis tells me you're quite a talent.

LEILA: Well I've always liked to sing.

BARNEY: Joe is what I like to call a friend of the establishment. There's nothing I wouldn't do for him. I was there when he brought justice to that Nazi Schmeling. I swear I cried with joy. What an American, huh? So what you gonna sing me?

LEILA: Well, um....

BARNEY: Don't be bashful, Miss. The stage is not a place to hide.

LEILA: Call me Leila.

BARNEY: In time.

LEILA: *(stalling)* Where's the accompanist?

BARNEY: What? Oh yeah, lemme call him. ISAAC!!

ISAAC reenters with milk.

BARNEY: Just tell us when you're ready. No pressure. Take your time, -- *(looks at his watch)* We got all the time in the world, --

LEILA: I'm fine!

BARNEY: Don't lemme rush ya, far be it from me to rush ya, --

LEILA: I'm ready. I just don't have any sheet music, --

BARNEY: You ever audition before?

LEILA: Of course I have. It's just, --

BARNEY: Just what? You can tell me.

LEILA: It's just I wasn't sure I'd have to sing.

BARNEY: You wanna do a tap instead?

LEILA: It's just that Joe said. He had it all arranged.

BARNEY: He did. He got you in the door. But the rest is up to you. If you're gonna get up on my stage, then I oughta know what you sound like. Or am I crazy?

LEILA: Guess I'm just naive.

BARNEY: You think I'm gonna hire ya just like that, you got another thing coming --

LEILA: I understand.

BARNEY: We understand each other. Okay. Now relax! Show me what you got.

ISAAC: *(at the piano)* Just start in babe, I'll catch up with ya.

LEILA: *(breathes, then)* I can sing most anything....But I'll give you one by a friend of mine....*(sings)* PALE MOON SHINING ON THE FIELDS BELOW//DARKIES CROONING SONGS SOFT AND LOW// NEEDN'T TELL ME SO BECAUSE I KNOW //IT'S SLEEPY TIME DOWN SOUTH *(confidence growing)* SOFT WIND BLOWING THROUGH THE PINEWOOD TREES//FOLKS DOWN THERE LIVE A LIFE OF EASE// WHEN OLD MAMMY FALLS UPON HER KNEES --

BARNEY: No no NO!!!

LEILA: What?

BARNEY: Stop. Please.

LEILA: What's wrong?

BARNEY: Everything.

LEILA: Sounds bad?

BARNEY: Not that.

LEILA: Then what?

BARNEY: Why you singing that song?

LEILA: Why?

BARNEY: Yeah, why?

LEILA: It's a good song.

BARNEY: You're a Negro woman. Aren't you a Negro woman?

LEILA: Yes, I'm a Neeegro wom--

BARNEY: Then what the hell ya singing a racist song like that for?

LEILA: Racist?

BARNEY: A Negro woman singing racist trash and she don't even know it! If that don't beat it.

LEILA: It's a popular song!

BARNEY: Racism is popular. That I can't deny.

LEILA: My friend is black! He's on the radio!

BARNEY: Amos or Andy?

ISAAC: Barney, --

BARNEY: Go eat your sandwich! *(to LEILA)* Listen. I got Billie Holliday here every Saturday. Josh White too twice a week. If I had 'em singing Sleepy Time Down South, I think they'd lynch me! *(beat)* No, no, no. This is definitely not what I'm looking for. Joe Louis is a friend of mine, but I can't fit you in if you pull stuff like this. Makes me wonder where's your self-respect!

LEILA: I did NOT come here for a lesson. This is not what I came here for.

BARNEY: Well you're gonna get one. You think I like doing this?

LEILA: Yes I do.

BARNEY: What a thing to say! I try to help this woman, --

LEILA: *(accent long gone by now)* Listen, Whitey. You couldn't help me if you tried. I'm a singer. A popular singer. I sing what's out there.

BARNEY: I know songs. I know what they mean.

LEILA: Maybe we gotta write some new songs. But right now this is what we got.

BARNEY: I hold you responsible for what you sing. Don't you understand? You wanna make it, you gotta show me who you are. Inside! You get me?

LEILA: (*changes tone*) Oh. You'd rather me sing the blues.

BARNEY: Well, yeah.

LEILA: A nice, sexy, hurting, victimized blues...like I'm sucking on your toes.... *(drops it)* Well I don't sing that kinda shit! I don't sing that to no white Jewish muthafucka wanna teach me self-respect. *(gets her coat)* Thanks Isaac. You got a nice touch.

BARNEY: Hold on.

LEILA: What else? You want me to wear a kerchief on my head?

BARNEY: I wanna give you a chance.

LEILA: Now you wanna give me a chance. Naw, I'm just an ign'rant li'l negress. I don't wanna waste your precious time.

BARNEY: You're wrong about the blues. Every country's got 'em. You oughta hear my cantor when he gets cooking. You gotta hear flamenco. Hell, even them Texas yodelers got a kind of blues. I don't sing myself. Never did. But I know blues. I care about the blues. It's passionate with me. And the Negro expression of the blues is what the people need to hear. Lemme speak for the audience. When they think of Negroes they see stevedores and Aunt Jemimas and washerwomen. But when I can get 'em in here to hear the blues -- well then they see people. Just people. Feeling what they feel. 'Cause people are real.

LEILA: But I don't want to be people.

BARNEY: Huh?

LEILA: I don't wanna be real. I am real. Twenty four hours a day I'm real. I want something better. *(beat)* I gotta go.

BARNEY: Wait -- *(holds his stomach)* Ooooh.

ISAAC: You all right, Boss?

BARNEY: Never better. Listen, Miss. Would you do me a favor? I know, you're saying to yourself, why should I? Well I'm asking. Would you sing me something? Any other goddamn song you want. But show me something, and I'll shut up! *(beat)* You gotta forgive me. I been seeing blues singers since you were a little girl. I see a dark woman like yourself, by the way the prettiest I seen, and I can't help but think, Boy, I bet she can really sing the blues. I dunno, something about the color of your skin. Anyway, that's just me. I want you to sing whatever you want, even Sleepy Time if you must. And I'll forget whose friend you are. From now on, it's just you and me. And Isaac. *(smiles)* You never know, Leila. You just might like it.

LEILA: Okay.

BARNEY: Okay then! Let's you and me be friends.

LEILA: You think?

BARNEY: Absolutely posilutely.

LEILA: No more racist songs for me, Sir. Thanks for pointing it out to me -- my mistake.

BARNEY: Not at all.

LEILA: I been swimming upstream long enough. Now I'm gonna give you want you want. *(to ISAAC)* You know that Peggy Lee tune? *(SINGS as he plays)* YOU HAD PLENTY MONEY 1922//YOU LET OTHER WOMEN MAKE A FOOL OF YOU// WHY DON'T YOU DO RIGHT//LIKE SOME OTHER MEN DO//GET OUTA HERE & GET ME SOME MONEY TOO

BARNEY: Oh yeah.

LEILA: *(sings)* YOU SITTING THERE WONDERING WHAT IT'S ALL ABOUT//YOU AIN'T GOT NO MONEY THEY WILL PUT YOU OUT //WHY DON'T YOU DO RIGHT// LIKE SOME OTHER MEN DO//GET OUTA HERE & GET ME SOME MONEY TOO//IF YOU HAD PREPARED TWENTY YEARS BEFORE//YOU WOULDN'T BE WANDERING NOW FROM

DOOR TO DOOR//WHY DON'T YOU DO RIGHT// LIKE
SOME OTHER MEN DO//GET OUTA HERE & GET ME SOME
MONEY TOO

BARNEY: Smile.

LEILA: WHY DON'T YOU DO RIGHT

BARNEY: Smile!

LEILA: LIKE SOME OTHER MEN DO

BARNEY: SMILE!

LEILA: LIKE SOME OTHER MEN DO?

END ACT ONE

ACT TWO

Scene 1
In semi-dark, the sound of RADIO STATIC. Hotel Room. Joe
playing with the radio dial.

ANNOUNCER: Bottom of the Seventh, 5 to 2, 1 out, DiMaggio at
the plate,....

Joe leans in listening. STATIC continues as we slowly we realize
that several radios are on at the same time.

ANNOUNCER 2: ...The immediate evacuation of all persons of
Japanese lineage,....

Joe leans in listening.

ANNOUNCER 3: This is Allistair Boag, live from the deck of the
Steamship Canonesa, en route from Buenos Aires to Liverpool --

He has three different-sized radios. He plays with the dials, trying
to get the best reception.

ANNOUNCER: A swing and a miss, --

Barney enters. Chocolate and flowers in his hand. Joe turns down
the VOLUME on each.

BARNEY: Say Joe! Who's winning?

JOE: Yankees.

BARNEY: Brooklyn hates the Bronx. When are the Dodgers
gonna finally knock 'em silly?

JOE: Gotta add a couple players.

BARNEY: From where?

JOE: Negro Leagues. *(off BARNEY's react)* Gotta happen
sometime.

BARNEY: Why not? We got a Jew or two in the Majors. Leila
here?

JOE: She putting on her face.

BARNEY: *(after a beat)* Sure got enough radios, Joe!

Joe turns up the volume on each radio dial.

ANNOUNCER: A high drive to left center field, --

ANNOUNCER 2: The Japanese race is an enemy race, --

JOE: I try to keep informed.

Joe turns two off. The third he switches to MUSIC.

JOE: Nothing against music.

BARNEY: *(listens)* Kay Keyser? And I thought all you liked was the blues.

JOE: Music is like a pretty girl. The world is blessed with a mess of 'em.

BARNEY: You really are some kinda individual.

JOE: I'm naturally curious.

BARNEY: Me too.

JOE: I know.

Joe smilingly stares Barney down.

BARNEY: *(clears throat)* Is it that obvious?

JOE: I won't tell.

BARNEY: I'm susceptible. My intentions are good -- I-I mean I don't wanna hurt nobody -- I-I mean --

JOE: We're men.

BARNEY: I can't help but ask...?

JOE: Leila?

BARNEY: I can help her. This business is all about who you

know, and how well you know 'em. But I don't wanna step outa bounds.

Joe shrugs good-naturedly. Barney coughs nervously.

BARNEY: You don't gotta say a word, Champ. I shouldn'ta brought it up, --

JOE: It's your business. Do what's right.

Leila enters, decked out.

LEILA: Barney.

BARNEY: You look like a million bucks.

LEILA: I'd rather have 'em.

Leila goes to Joe expecting an embrace. Gracefully but firmly Joe avoids contact. Leila regains her equilibrium.

LEILA: Joe, I'm not sure when we'll be back --

JOE: Take your time. *(holds up his wrist)* I don't wear a watch.

BARNEY: You're not coming?

JOE: I gotta make a living.

Leila looks at him. His behavior seems oddly familiar.

BARNEY: *(shakes JOE's hand)* I wouldn't trade ya for a two pitchers and an outfielder.

LEILA: Joe?

JOE: Hit a homerun, girl.

Leila approaches. He eludes her. No physical contact will occur with Barney in the room. She sniffs.

LEILA: You gonna be here when I get back?

JOE: *(smiles)* I'll be back.

Barney puts her coat on her shoulders. She leaves the chocolates.

They exit. Silence. Joe turns on the radio.

Scene 2

In semi-dark the opening strains of "DON'T CRY BABY."

ANNOUNCER: Live from the Mocha Club in downtown Manhattan, we are pleased to bring you fifteen minutes of authentic Negro jazz and blues. Tonight, making her debut, is Li'l Leila Rivers and "Cry Baby"....

Leila appears in spotlight, made-up, forced smile on her face, nervous. One cue, she launches in.

LEILA: *(sings)* DON'T CRY BABY//DON'T CRY BABY//DRY YOUR EYES//LET'S BE SWEETHEARTS AGAIN//YOU KNOW I DIDN'T MEAN//TO EVER TREAT YOU SO MEAN//COME ON SWEETHEART//LET'S START OVER AGAIN

As the band takes over, she sighs with relief. Pastes the smile on one last time. Leila leads the band. She is gaining confidence with every second. As she readies to sing, --

We see Joe Louis training. Works up a sweat. Radio on.

In a separate space we see Demas Dean pressing pants at the Tailor Shop, listening also to the radio.

LEILA: DON'T CRY, DON'T CRY//LITTLE BABY DON'T YOU CRY

First Demas, then Joe, recognizes Leila on the radio.

LEILA: CAUSE YOUR MOMMY'S COMING HOME//JUST AS SURE AS YOU'RE BORN//SO DON'T YOU CRY *(smile of triumph)* BABY DON'T YOU CRY

As the song ends, spot out on Leila. Out on Demas and the Tailor Shop. Lights up on Joe Louis in his Pompton Lakes training camp. He jumps rope. He seems exquisitely alone.

ACCOUNTANT enters. BELL rings. Accountant throws him a towel.

JOE: Thanks.

ACCOUNTANT: Don't mention it. Looking swell, Champ.

JOE: Feel pretty good.

ACCOUNTANT: You're in for a fight. Abe Simon's a big man.

JOE: Plenty tough too.

ACCOUNTANT: Smart money's on you. Same as always. *(smells the air)* Sure is beautiful out here. You forget you're in Jersey.

JOE: I like the quiet. *(shakes his head)* The City,....

ACCOUNTANT: Distracting?

JOE: You might say.

ACCOUNTANT: Expensive?

JOE: That too.

ACCOUNTANT: Not to mention the girls.

JOE: Don't mention 'em.

ACCOUNTANT: Got any trouble?

JOE: No trouble.

ACCOUNTANT: That's right. You're a married man.

BELL rings.

JOE: It ain't tax time, is it?

ACCOUNTANT: It's always tax time. We gotta talk, Joe.

JOE: What's the damage? *(off ACCOUNTANT's smile)* Go on. I can take it.

ACCOUNTANT: Well Champ, the Internal Revenue Service as assessed your last year's earnings, and your tax bill amounts to $117,000.

JOE: Pay it.

ACCOUNTANT: You don't got the money. *(beat)* Fortunately, since you joined the Army, you won't have to pay till the war's over.

JOE: Ain't I lucky.

ACCOUNTANT: I don't know about that.

JOE: Couple big fights do the trick.

ACCOUNTANT: *(with portfolio)* Well, I've been trying to make some sense of your debts. I have here that you owe your promoter somewhere close to $60,000. You owe your management team at least $60,000 more. Then, as for training expenses, namely here at Pompton Lakes, you owe upwards on --

JOE: Hold on. You saying I can't pay those neither?

ACCOUNTANT: Not unless you hit the numbers today. Shall I go on?

JOE: I think I get the picture. How come I didn't know about this before?

ACCOUNTANT: Well you do now. *(beat)* Your record-keeping has been unorthodox to say the least.

JOE: I pay you to keep 'em.

ACCOUNTANT: I'm not a clerk, Champ. And I didn't blow the cash. *(beat)* So what are we gonna do?

JOE: I don't know what you're gonna do, but I got to get this thing paid off....

ACCOUNTANT: That's what I'm really here about, --

JOE: All's I needs a couple big fights.

ACCOUNTANT: I've been in touch with the War Department on precisely this issue. It hasn't hit the papers yet, but it seems that Secretary of War Stimson --

JOE: Stimson, yeah, he the one got me to give up my purse to War Relief. Got me to join up too --

ACCOUNTANT: Well Stimson says that --

JOE: He can have some money too. I just wanna pay my debt.

ACCOUNTANT: Right, but --

JOE: Billy Conn. Talk about tough. Then Bob Pastor again or Jimmy Bivins. Galento maybe, Mauriello, -- hey I'll take 'em on one a month till we --

ACCOUNTANT: Stimson says you can't fight anymore. *(beat)* The reason being, it's not fair for you to work off your debts while in the service of your country. Uncle Sam doesn't believe in special treatment for anybody. Sorry.

BELL rings.

JOE: This mean I can't fight Simon?

ACCOUNTANT: Oh no, the Simon fight stands. Navy Relief needs your donation. Money's already spent.

JOE: Lemme fight some more, I'll make us all a buncha cash, --

ACCOUNTANT: War Relief says you can fight when the War's over. I think you're gonna need to.

JOE: I need to fight now.

ACCOUNTANT: Decision's final. *(beat)* So. I recommend you enjoy your term in the military. Chances are you'll tour with the USO. *(imagines them)* Betty Grable? Lana Turner -- Boy! Sure pays to be a celebrity!

JOE: I'm a fighter.

ACCOUNTANT: Not anymore, Champ. Not unless you wanna fight for free. *(thinks)* Actually that's a possibility. Stimson recommends a series of exhibitions, real good for morale and what have you --

JOE: What about the title?

ACCOUNTANT: Frozen.

JOE: You telling me this is my last fight?

ACCOUNTANT: Except.... *(a gleam in his eye)* Except of course if Simon were to win.

JOE: How do you mean?

ACCOUNTANT: Don't quote me now, let's just say a little bird told me. And don't get me wrong, Champ. You've been a credit to your race. But somebody like Abe Simon could really help the War effort. I mean, he's a big American square-jawed apple-pie kinda guy. We're looking for a symbol. Something we can win with.

JOE: Abe Simon?

ACCOUNTANT: Well he's the only one still standing. *(confidential)* Look Champ. We're not suggesting anything improper -- heck no! But I talked to the bigwigs at the Revenue Service, and they told me -- well -- those numbers are negotiable.

JOE: *(quietly resolute)* Abe Simon a strong man. I don't grudge him nothing. But he want my title, he gotta take it from me. I know what you saying. But I got people out there pulling for me. They want me to win. It gives me strength.

ACCOUNTANT: Sure, they love ya. They'll always love ya, Champ. But we're talking about your country here. This is bigger than your fans, this is --

JOE: No. I'm just about the biggest thing they got.

ACCOUNTANT: We're talking about a lotta money here.

JOE: So you tell me.

ACCOUNTANT: I don't think you understand. You're in some deep water. I've a good mind to let you drown, --!

JOE: I'll pay it back if it takes me the rest of my natural life, --

ACCOUNTANT: That can be arranged.

BELL rings.

ACCOUNTANT: Do you have any idea who you're dealing with?

JOE: No. Thanks for dropping by. I won't be needing your services anymore.

ACCOUNTANT: Are you kidding? I'm your lifeline! I'm the only one can get you outa this jam!

JOE: It's my jam.

ACCOUNTANT: Then it's outa my hands. *(starts to exit)* There's a lotta people watching, Joe. And they ain't only fight fans.

Accountant exits. Joe stands in limbo.

ANNOUNCER: We're at Madison Square Garden only hours from the main event between Champion Joe Louis and Big Abe Simon. Tonight's fracas will be short-waved all over the free world in the biggest radio hook-up since boxing began. The Mutual Broadcast System wants every soldier in every outpost from the Philippines to North Africa to hear the fight. At the weigh-in today, Abe scaled 255 pounds. Joe came in at 207, a little on the heavy side for him. Well, if training camp didn't get him in tip-top shape, then the Army will.

Joe jolted into wakefulness, exits.

Scene 3

Van approaches House. Wears the same now ratty suit, but his shoes are still shiny.

VAN : My luck gone a little south on me, ever since that little Brooklyn harpy done her shuck and jive downtown. Always said she was a witch. *(beat)* How deep am I into you? *(off HOUSE's react)* That deep? Well that's just the way I got it planned. You don't t'ink I can pull this off. I can see it in your eyes. You think I'll fall apart like the rest of 'em. But I ain't cocking this up. If the number don't hit, the dog dead. And I don't want the dog to die. *(pulls out an envelope)* The club and everything in it. *(grins)* I gonna break the bank with this hit. House, tomorrow you'll be broke solid. *(beat)* Real blabbermouth, ain't ya.

House rises.

HOUSE: House don't got to speak.

As Van exits, --

Scene 4

In semi-dark, --

ANNOUNCER: Joe Louis still champeen! Is there a man out there who can stop him? Joe knocked out Big Abe Simon last evening for the twenty-first defense of his title. This morning three of the Negro community's biggest and brightest stars announced a collaboration to honor the brightest star of them all. Paul Robeson, Count Basie, and Richard Wright will come together this weekend to record a new popular blues celebrating the life and career of Private First Class Joe Louis Barrow. You can bet, if it's a blues about King Joe, then it's bound to swing and pack a punch like a mule! Congrats, Joe! Not only are you a credit to your race -- You're the King of them all! *(alters the radio voice)* Now it's time for the weekly broadcast live from the Mocha Club, bringing you the latest in popular hits of the blues variety, and featuring...Hazel Scott!

Leila turns the radio off.

LEILA: Hazel Scott? She can't sing, --

Leila faces us as in a mirror. Hair done up in a towel. On the table are several pharmeceutical vials. On her lap is a bowl into which she's creating a creamy substance.

Sound of a toilet flush, then Joe appears, moving slow and in some pain. Undresses down to tanktop and shorts.

LEILA: Still bleeding?

JOE: Sure can hit. *(nods at the radio)* How come you ain't at the club?

LEILA: I need a week's preparation.

JOE: What you got there?

LEILA: Beauty secrets.

JOE: You don't need none. *(beat)* Got something to eat? Fry me up a chicken.

LEILA: I don't do meals.

JOE: Some wife you'd make.

LEILA: Say what?

JOE: Just kidding.

LEILA: How many wives you wanna have?

JOE: I didn't mean it like that.

LEILA: You wanna meal, go home and let your wife cook you one.

JOE: She don't cook.

LEILA: Then get the maid.

JOE: She don't cook Southern.

LEILA: Then get your mother.

JOE: She is Michigan.

LEILA: Well there's a Carolina greasy spoon down the corner. Don't look at me.

JOE: *(RE: the bowl)* What's that stuff? Can I eat it?

LEILA: Probably tastes better than it works.

JOE: *(reading the vials)* Borax? Hydrous Wool Fat? Am-Amon-moniated Mercury --?

LEILA: Put that on top your grits.

JOE: Smell strong.

Dabs cream onto a cloth, then covers her face with it.

JOE: Burn?

LEILA: I can take it.

JOE: Come on. Take that stuff off and come to bed. I ain't seen you since training camp. Come on. Take it off.

LEILA: Get your hands off!

JOE: I don't like that stuff.

LEILA: Get your goddamn hands off!

JOE: What is it? Smells like -- like --

LEILA: Think about it.

JOE: This is bleach.

LEILA: Let's just hope it works.

JOE: How long you been doing this?

LEILA: Not long enough.

JOE: How long?

LEILA: A week.

JOE: But you so fine-looking, --

LEILA: It ain't gonna change my face. I just got too much color.

JOE: You got a pretty color, --

LEILA: I got too much of it. Dark don't win no favors. Dark is fat,
ignorant, and victimized.

JOE: But you was born dark, --

LEILA: So, you was born poor. You did something about it.

JOE: But you a black woman.

LEILA: I'm a singer. And if this works, I'm gonna make movies.
And movies stars ain't no darker than a suntan. I ain't gonna be no
Jemima. Few shades lighter I'll pass for Mexican.

JOE: But you ain't.

LEILA: You can talk. You got a light color yourself.

JOE: This the way I come out.

LEILA: Think if you was one of them Black African types. Bet you wouldn't be champ. You'da never got the shot. *(beat)* Me I'm doing something about it. Dark folk sing the blues, that's why they call 'em darkies. Look Egyptian, they let you swing with Benny Goodman.

JOE: Please don't do it.

LEILA: *(shows an arm or leg)* You think this is fine? It ain't ain't worth shit. This little negress ain't worth shit the way she is.

JOE: I said, don't do it.

LEILA: *(applying more)* I'm supposed to stop 'cause the Big Man tell me to? Shit. Why dontcha give me some of that money you gave Army Relief last night?

JOE: You asked me. Did I ever hate? And I answered no. Well that weren't true. 'Cause if there's one thing I do hate it's -- it's --

LEILA: What? A li'l negress tryna be white?

JOE: You can't be.

LEILA: Can't be what? White? I'd rather DIE than be white. I wish I didn't have any color! Wish I didn't have a face at all!!!

JOE: Please. Be who you are.

LEILA: I can't support myself the way I am. *(beat)* RCA Victor turned me down. Too inexperienced. Yeah, right. Now the radio people giving me shit.

JOE: Can't Barney help?

LEILA: He's in love with about three other black women. I ain't got time to wait on him. I got to make my breaks. *(beat)* I could use some money. *(no answer)* I said I could use some cash. *(still no answer)* You said you'd take care of me!

JOE: I can't just now.

LEILA: Why the hell not?

JOE: I'm a little broke just now.

LEILA: So make some money.

JOE: Not just now.

LEILA: You're the champ! What good's the title for anyway if you can't make any money off it?!! *(no answer)* It's this goddamn war, isn't it.

Joe removes an envelope.

JOE: Draft Board. Report to Camp Upton. I don't even know where that is.

LEILA: Ain't that bad. Officers make good pay.

JOE: Officer?

LEILA: Don't tell me you gonna be a Private?

JOE: I turned down officer. I just wanna be with my people.

LEILA: Cleaning latrines?

JOE: I'm a fighter.

LEILA: They got you right where they want you.

JOE: I just wanna do my duty.

LEILA: *(applying cream)* Another tribe.

JOE: I love my people.

LEILA: I swear, they oughta let the women fight. I'd kick some ass.

JOE: All I want....

LEILA: Go on, say it.

JOE: All I want is....

LEILA: Another sob story?

JOE: All I want is a nice big bed and some chicken!!

LEILA: *(laughs)* You can't be that broke!

JOE: I just wanna eat and sleep and do my job! I don't wanna do bad! I tried -- *(breaks down)*

LEILA: Aw man.

JOE: I swear I tried. But nobody look out for me. How am I supposed to look out for you? I can't look out for you. You got to go your own way.

LEILA: I already have.

JOE: Shoulda stayed wit' your horn player.

They are on the floor in a semi-pieta.

JOE: Nobody look out for me....Why don't nobody look out for me...?

LEILA: I know why. *(beat)* You gotta lose somehow.

As she strokes his hair, --

Scene 5

SOUTHERN TAILOR SHOP. Demas presses a suit, tape measure around his neck. Sidney cooks red beans and rice.

DEMAS: *(hums, then)* How's it go again?

SIDNEY: You know Basie, liable to come up with something mighty different, but last night it sounded something like this.

Sidney hums the tune to "KING JOE, THE JOE LOUIS BLUES."

DEMAS: Pretty straight up.

SIDNEY: Keep it simple, play it gentle.

DEMAS: Really the blues. *(hums double time)* Got me a tune of my own. Help me out.

SIDNEY: Got any woids?

DEMAS: Do I got any woids. *(sings, slaps his thigh)* HE'S STILL THE KING OF THEM ALL//HE'S STILL THE KING OF THEM ALL//OL' JOE LOUIS// HE'S STILL THE KING OF THEM ALL *(raps 40s style)* HE MADE A HADDOCK OUT BRADDOCK//A RUG OUTA BAER//BOSTON JACK SHARKEY JUST GOT NOWHERE BILLY CONN HE WAS GONE//ABE SIMON TOO//AND GALENTO AND SCH'MELIN' COME OUT BLACK AND BLUE *(hits stride)* HE TOOK ON ALL COMERS//HE FOUGHT 'EM CLEAN//THE OL' BROWN BOMBER WAS A FIGHTING MACHINE//HE JAB WITH THE LEFT --

SIDNEY: UGH!

DEMAS: JAB WITH A RIGHT --

SIDNEY: UGH!

DEMAS: THEN COME THE UPPERCUT --

SIDNEY/DEMAS: STOP THAT FIGHT!!!

DEMAS: HE'S STILL THE KING OF THEM ALL

SIDNEY: HE'S STILL THE KING OF THEM ALL

DEMAS: THAT OL' JOE LOUIS//HE'S STILL THE KING

SIDNEY: THE KING OF THE RING

DEMAS: THE CHAMP OF CHAMPS//JOE LOUIS!!!!

They slap five.

Van enters during the song. Jaunty, grinning.

SIDNEY: Monsieur Vantyle! Where y'at?

VAN: I'm right where I want to be. Mm-mmn-mmn! I smell somet'ing --!

SIDNEY: Come to mooch my vittles!!

VAN: Caught your whiff a block away. *(nods to DEAN)* Hey Dean.

DEMAS: *(nods back)* Hey old man. *(they slap five)* No hard feelings.

VAN: Where you fine suit, King?

DEMAS: Now I make 'em. That's a fine suit, man. Too bad you wore it to death.

VAN: That what it for.

DEMAS: Oughta show your threads more respect. Like people. Treat 'em half-way decent, maybe you won't look so bad.

VAN: T'anks for the tip. Making suits now -- I got to stop calling you Cornet King.

DEMAS: I'm not giving up the music.

VAN: Ain't playing, is ya?

DEMAS: From what I hear the club's going downhill fast.

VAN: My money elsewhere.

DEMAS: Coming up short, huh?

VAN: Dean, I do somet'ing, I do it all the way.

DEMAS: Well, WHEN you hit, Sidney and me'll suit you up with something fine to fit a man of means.

VAN: Why you t'ink I'm here?

Pause.

DEMAS: Huh?

VAN: Put that tape to good use, man. I want your best suit!

DEMAS: Oh my god!! You did it!!

VAN: I'm de Champ!!! *(dances with joy)*

DEMAS: Hot damn!! Holy Moly I been wrong about you!! Say Bash! I can't believe it!! This brother here, he hit it! He hit the bigtime!!

SIDNEY: *(comes running)* Course he did!!

DEMAS: I didn't think you could!! But you did it --!!!

VAN: **Tonight**, Dean.

All festivities stop.

VAN: TONIGHT. I can feel it in my bones. *(still talking big)* Foolproof. I got the angle this time. Be the biggest hit in history. T'ought I'd help you boys out. Give you my good business. Well?

Uneasy pause.

SIDNEY: Don't got to tell me twice. Start up a credit line for de big Bossman.

Silent, Demas measures Van for a new suit.

VAN: I was thinking a conservative cut. What Rockefeller wearing these days?

SIDNEY: He's zooting it up with the best of 'em. Wall Street grey'ud suit ya fine. We got shoes too. Florsheims. We call 'em ghetto cadillacs. Like crazy.

VAN: Shoes make de man. *(offhand)* Word on the street is, you boys gonna cut a record.

SIDNEY: Tonight.

DEMAS: *Joe Louis Blues*.

Sidney returns to cooking.

VAN: You too, Dean?

DEMAS: Bash been looking out for me.

VAN: But why the blues? Why not the Joe Louis Swing?

DEMAS: Ain't no dance tune. You supposed to listen.

VAN: Who got time to listen?

DEMAS: You supposed to make the time.

VAN: *(laughs)* Never happen.

DEMAS: Richard Wright. Paul Robeson. Count Basie.

VAN: Got a novelist try to write blues, a concert singer try to sing it, and a Kansas City hick try to swing it. Least you get paid. *(trying to act offhand)* Bet you get a nice little paycheck.

DEMAS: Ain't a question of that.

VAN: But you do get paid.

DEMAS: I guess.

VAN: I swear. This hit be for all of us.

SIDNEY: Whatchu gonna do with all that cash?

DEMAS: First thing he gonna pay me for this suit.

Sidney gives Van some homecooking.

SIDNEY: Line your flue with this. The *specialite*.

VAN: *(eats)* Whoo -- my tongue on fire!!!

Demas hears something on the radio. Announcer appears.

DEMAS: Hush up now --!!

ANNOUNCER: It's official! Joe Louis out of boxing! For the duration of the War, Joe Louis has pledged to hang up his gloves and set aside his title belt. There's a bigger fight now and we're all in it. Hitler Beware!! The Brown Bomber says you can run but you can't hide!!

Demas flicks it off in despair. Announcer disappears.

DEMAS: Doggone it!!

SIDNEY: It'll be all right.

DEMAS: Doggone this war!!

VAN: *(laughs alone)* Pretty soon it'll be your turn, Dean. Maybe you can dig a trench with Private Joe. Got yer draft notice yet?

SIDNEY: Not yet.

VAN: Better buy yerself a bulletproof union suit.

SIDNEY: He don't need to hear that.

VAN: Want my advice? Burn your birt' certificate. Poof! Like you was never even born!

SIDNEY: You may know numbers, Bossman. But you don't know shit about dodging authority. Me, I been doing that most of my natural life.

VAN: Then what your big idea? How you gonna get your boy off de hook? Become a reefer addict? Go fruity? What?

DEMAS: Tell me, Bash.

Sidney checks to make sure no one is listening in.

SIDNEY: Join the Post Office. *(VAN guffaws)* No jive. Go on out to California and join the Post Office, Demas. Army ain't gonna draft no federal employee, not yet anyway. Hopefully this war thing be over 'fore too long anyhow.

VAN: You outa your mind, Bechet.

SIDNEY: You know what else? Get married.

VAN: Get married? Ha!!

DEMAS: I want to.

VAN: To whom, Leila? Anybody but Li'l Leila!!

DEMAS: Why you gotta bring her up?!!

SIDNEY: Calm down, Boy.

DEMAS: I'll kill the fucka --!!

SIDNEY: *(holds him back)* Don't mess up. *(avuncular to DEMAS)* You shoulda called her.

DEMAS: She don't wanna hear from me.

VAN: *(still laughing)* Li'l Leila!!

DEMAS: I gotta get outa here. Meet you at the gig, Bash. *(face to face with VAN)* Sorry, Van. But I just can't feature you no more.

Demas exits.

SIDNEY: He ain't a boy no more. You keep it up, he'll kick your ass. *(beat)* So what you got?

VAN: Mezz was a little late with the stash.

SIDNEY: I unnerstand. *(removes a box of mezzrolls)* Always keep a bit in reserve.

VAN: The master himself!

SIDNEY: Care for a hit? *(VAN demurs, SIDNEY tokes)* You in trouble, ain't ya.

VAN: *(struggles)* How 'bout a little loan?

SIDNEY: You hocked everything? The club too?

VAN: You get rich wit' me!

SIDNEY: I don't need riches.

VAN: I do. *(hand out)* How 'bout it, my friend?

SIDNEY: Never thought I'd see the day you'd be asking me for cash.

Sidney pulls out his wad of cash.

VAN: You ain't be sorry!! What you know, Sidney?!!

SIDNEY: Man, I don't know nothing.

VAN: I find you tonight, when you done recording. We have a few on me. Wine, women and song! I come back a rich man!

Van exits fast out the door.

SIDNEY: Just make sure you hit.

Sidney alone, eats and smokes.

Has just taken a long hit when Leila enters.

SIDNEY: Well hey beautiful! *(they hug)* You honor me.

LEILA: I missed your dirty rice and beans.

SIDNEY: Well I love you too. Hoid you in the rahdio. Mighty proud.

LEILA: I quit.

SIDNEY: Say what?

LEILA: Sonsabitches pulled me off the broadcast. Said I didn't sing enough blues.

SIDNEY: What about that Barney fella?

LEILA: Today he tells me he got a new girl for my show. Asks me do I want to lead the band.

SIDNEY: Uh-oh. You didn't lose your temper?

LEILA: I didn't lose nothing. *(her fist)* Right in the nose. Think I broke it.

SIDNEY: Oh baby, you can't just go bopping people on the head. Not your bigtime managers no how, that'll be a hard one to live down --

LEILA: I don't wanna live it down. I'm through.

SIDNEY: With the music?

LEILA: I feel so goddamned alone. I look in the shop windows, I can't see myself.

SIDNEY: Don't quit.

LEILA: My life's getting a little crispy around the edges.

SIDNEY: Baby, that's the tastiest part.

LEILA: *Sleepy Time Down South*...remember?

SIDNEY: Sure.

LEILA: You know the words?

SIDNEY: Can't say I do. Why?

LEILA: Part of my education. Useta think the blues were racist. Now I wonder if the whole damn thing is rotten.

SIDNEY: It gets mean, Girl. But not the music. It's a road. There's good things. There's miseries. The road keeps going. You can stop, but it don't. It's the thing that brings you to everything else. You got to trust that. No one ever came back who can't tell you that.

LEILA: That's a buncha words.

SIDNEY: The way I see it you ain't even on the road yet. Yeah, you sound good and you look fine. But you ain't no musicianeer. Not yet. Not even close.

LEILA: Then I did right quitting.

SIDNEY: Ain't I never tell you about my dog Goola?!!

LEILA: No.

SIDNEY: See, I was ignorant too. I called him Goola. But I meant Gullah.

LEILA: Gullah?

SIDNEY: It's a backwoods way of speaking. Real musical. What the Africans useta talk when they got brung here. Still talk it, but quiet-like. When I was far away, real far from home, I useta miss that sound. That beautiful sound. See, I wanted to keep that Gullah with me, no matter where I went. No matter what kinda shit went down -- and you know a lot did. But I had that sound,....

LEILA: What sound?

SIDNEY: Call it a memory. Somebody begins to sing. Simple, like the old folks do, like a chant,....

Sidney starts to hum, then to chant.

SIDNEY:And you can feel it grow, and the song comes by itself, makes you wanna move, to chant, and we bring it all back....

Sidney sings, more sounds than words, something older than blues and deeper than anything written, rocking in rhythm, his body a musical instrument.

SIDNEY: Bringing back who we really are.

LEILA: Who are we?

SIDNEY: A great people from a long ways away.

LEILA: I never been there.

The sounds have created a sexuality in the air.

SIDNEY: Lemme take you there, --

LEILA: No --

SIDNEY: I'm gonna call you, --

LEILA: Sidney --

SIDNEY: It's right here.

LEILA: You been smoking your brain.

SIDNEY: Yeah but that don't mean nothing.

LEILA: I love you, but I don't want this. I been following one man or another as long as I can remember. I don't want no Gullah. I ain't gonna do no run-an-fetch. I gotta find a song for now.

Sidney slowly comes out of his trance.

SIDNEY: Just don't quit.

LEILA: Who's quitting.

Leila at the door. She's seems stronger, more together.

SIDNEY: What should I tell Demas?

LEILA: Tell him be ready. 'Cause it ain't over yet.

SIDNEY: Leila --

Leila exits fast. Sidney takes a hit on the mezzroll but the joint has gone out.

Scene 6

MUSIC -- an amazing Bechet blues sax riff.

Spot on Joe in front of a mirror, putting on his uniform, taking his time. His expression difficult to penetrate. But the music makes Joe smile.

RECORDING STUDIO. Demas enters with cornet as Sidney finishes the blues riff LIVE. Barney and Announcer stride by. Sure enough, Barney's nose is bandaged in a splint, his eyes swollen.

ANNOUNCER: Testing. One-two-three --

BARNEY: Will ya stand still a minute? This is business!

ANNOUNCER: No. Tonight's about Joe.

BARNEY: Sure, but business just doesn't stop! Certainly don't stop for you radio guys! Now look. Gimme another chance. Don't pull the plug on my broadcast!

DEMAS: Did you know you was the dead image of Beethoven?

SIDNEY: Ludwig is a friend of mine.

ANNOUNCER: Hey, it'all about the bottom line. The people want to hear the hottest new talent on the scene. And the Mocha Club ain't cutting it.

BARNEY: You're going with the Cafe Society?!!

ANNOUNCER: Billie Holliday's packing 'em in, Barn.

BARNEY: That sheister Josephson stole her from under my nose!!

ANNOUNCER: In a manner of speaking.

BARNEY: You guys at CBS gotta give us another shot. Come on, be a pal!

ANNOUNCER: Don't ask me, I just read what they put in fronta me.

BARNEY: Listen. I got a gal who could make a bundle. She's a bit hot-headed, but --

ANNOUNCER: *(gesturing at the nose)* So she's the one --?

Their conversation continues as they move to one side.

DEMAS: Been thinking about that advice you give me. *(a sheaf of papers)* Postal application.

SIDNEY: No jive!

DEMAS: I'm gonna do it. *(beat)* I'm going to California too. Get about as far away from Peaches as I can.

SIDNEY: Now that's funny, 'cause guess who come by looking for you, --

ANNOUNCER: *(takes the stand-up mike)* Right fellas. Soon as Misters Basie and Robeson show up, we can all get down to business --

SIDNEY: Try the corner bar, Basie'd be late to his own funeral.

ANNOUNCER: Hope you're all good and warm.

SIDNEY: We cooking.

ANNOUNCER: Just wanted to take this moment to introduce the man of the hour who is here on a one-night pass -- the King of Them All -- Joe Louis.

Applause as Joe enters in uniform.

ANNOUNCER: Well Joe, it's our intention to celebrate your life and what you mean to this country of ours. There isn't a man who's not proud of you and what you've done.

Joe steps up. Humble, gentle.

JOE: Thanks. I just wanna say -- thanks. 'Cause I tried to be a good man. It's hard -- life can be hard -- but you all know that. In this life you learn a lot of things. But thanks for looking out for me.

Applause, they think he's finished. He waits.

JOE: Guess I'll be good soldier over there. But the real fight,...Well, I think it's here. It's up to you. It's a good fight. And,...Thank you.

He steps away.

ANNOUNCER: We'll do what we can, Joe. (*to the assemblage*) Five minutes, everybody.

Joe is surrounded by Barney, Announcer and whoever else. Demas rises and interrupts.

DEMAS: Excuse me.

ANNOUNCER: Didn't catch your name.

DEMAS: Dean. Demas Dean.

ANNOUNCER: Well Dean, thanks for being here. Now listen Champ --

DEMAS: *(to JOE)* You remember Leila Rivers?

JOE: Yeah.

Barney reacts.

DEMAS: Listen, uh....

JOE: You the horn player.

DEMAS: You remember.

JOE: Hey, I'm sorry.

DEMAS: Sorry?

JOE: Wish I could do something. I feel real bad about the way things worked out --

DEMAS: You didn't do nothing wrong --

JOE: Yeah I did.

ANNOUNCER: *(tries to give them room)* Come on, Barn, let's us be moving on --

BARNEY: Hold on a minute --

DEMAS: You ain't with her no more? *(JOE shakes his head no)* So you ain't with her!!

JOE: I'm a married man. *(extends a hand)* Good luck. She's one tough woman.

BARNEY: She's vicious!!

Joe double-takes. Demas still shakes his hand.

DEMAS: Joe...when they send you out to fight....Don't get shot.

JOE: I'll try not to.

DEMAS: Don't get shot. Just don't get shot.

JOE: I'll be back.

DEMAS: I'll be waiting.

Leila enters. Everything stops. Leila looks from one man to the other. Bechet, Barney, Joe, Demas.

Leila takes Demas's hand and leads him away from the others.

DEMAS: Jeez.

LEILA: Come on.

BARNEY: Now wait just a minute --!!

Leila turns on Barney, sends him flinching in retreat.

DEMAS: What you doing here?

LEILA: You're lucky I'm back. Come on.

She tries to lead him off.

DEMAS: I can't.

LEILA: I ain't waiting.

DEMAS: But we gotta do Joe's blues.

LEILA: You don't gotta do nothing. Leastwise for Joe.

DEMAS: Yes I do.

LEILA: Why? He shits like the next man, steps in it same as anyone. Why play a song for him? Play a song for him, play one for me too!

DEMAS: Maybe one day we will. But tonight we play for him.

LEILA: I came to offer you...a proposition.

DEMAS: What?

LEILA: Look, I know you still want me. And I don't know where else to go just now. So let's make a deal. Let's you and me settle.

DEMAS: Settle?

LEILA: Yeah. Married, single, whatever.

DEMAS: Jeez. *(melting)* Wouldya --? Couldya?

LEILA: Let's go.

DEMAS: Oh man! Gonna be great in California!

LEILA: California's out. *(DEMAS stops)* We're staying right here.

DEMAS: I gotta go.

LEILA: Not in the plan.

DEMAS: What plan?

LEILA: I didn't get what I wanted, why should you? *(beat)* Look. Why keep fighting if you're just gonna lose? That's something I learned from you. *(takes his hand)* See what I mean? We're made for each other.

DEMAS: *(extricates his hand)* No. We're not.

LEILA: What the hell --?

DEMAS: I got a gig to play.

LEILA*: (face contorting)* Goddamn Geechee dirtblack NIGGERS—

Leila exits in a fury.

BARNEY: Hey Leila! I oughta take you to court*! (to the OTHERS)* Some chick, huh? I tell you, she's gonna be somebody,....

As lights fade, for the first time we hear the rather monotone "THE JOE LOUIS BLUES" sung by a rather stiff Paul Robeson. As it plays, --

Demas appears in semi-dark, cradling his cornet.

DEMAS: I don't know why. We couldn'ta played with more love if we tried. But that song is a dud. Coupla times ol' Paul Robeson nearly caught fire, but it was kinda like wet kindling. What'd we do wrong, Bash?

Sidney alongside him, sax in one hand, weed in the other.

SIDNEY: Not a thing, Boy.

DEMAS: Ain't it a bad song?

SIDNEY: Yep, but it come from a good place. It ain't the song. It's where you take it. Where it takes you. I don't regret a thing.

DEMAS: Then what happened?

SIDNEY: We on a slow blind curve of the road. Can't see what's in front of us, can't see behind neither. Least we on the road.
DEMAS: How about Leila? She on the road too?

SIDNEY: I don't know. *(beat)* Maybe she making a new road.

DEMAS: Where she gonna go?

SIDNEY: One never knows. Do one.

DEMAS: I dodged a bullet tonight, Bash. But I kinda feel like maybe I made a mistake getting outa the way.

SIDNEY: How can it be a mistake? You love who you love, Boy. *(kisses his sax)* You love who you love. That's what the song is all about.

As they exit, --

Scene 7

Blackbird. Van appears with a suitcase. House on the barstool. Van places the envelope on the bar.

VAN: Bible never say "It came to stay." It say "It came to pass."

House says nothing. Puts it in his coat pocket. Exits. Van watches him go. Drinks deep.

VAN: *(toasts)* Goodbye, Darkietown!

Leila enters through the beads. She has been crying.

VAN: Well if it ain't the Devil's own rag babydoll.

LEILA: This place stinks of cheap slop.

VAN: So it does. Cheap slop and African funk. Now don't tell me! You come back for your old job?!! Swing your ass for Sleepy Time blackfolk? Friends is friends, woman. But you want it, I have to audition you.

LEILA: I don't want your filthy job!

VAN: Ha! Oh yeah! You a hot commodity!

LEILA: Just quit it.

VAN: Lady on fire 'cause she show some skin in Crackertown!

LEILA: I told you to LAY OFF!! *(beat)* I came 'cause I'm tired. Don't you ever get tired?

VAN: Black man tired all the time.

LEILA: My body hurts. Like I got punched in the guts. I just want a little peace. I didn't know where else to go.

VAN: I know why you here. You come to see the nigger people.

LEILA: Get away from me. Broke one man's nose already today. Don't get me started.

VAN: You like my face? Black enough for ya?

LEILA: Goddamn you, shiftless bluegum sonofa--

VAN: I know why you back. You can't pass. No wonder you tired. Ain't light enough. I coulda told you that. Black girl too funky for de swells downtown. So you come back to home base. The jungle. Darkietown! Wanna be a goodtime geechee tarbaby like de old days --

LEILA: *(tries to slug him)* Sonofabitch!!

VAN: Tell me it ain't true, Geechee Gumbo!!

LEILA: All right, muthafucka. I'm back for one last look. One last look at this hellhole and you, you piss-ant piece of West Indian trash. One last look, then I'm gone. You hear me? Gone. Escaped. Poof! Thin air. Next time you see me, it'll be on the screen. Singing my black ass off for the big bucks. You'll see the whole pretty package, shaking it like it's going outa style, only now it'll be lookee but no touchee, 'cause I'll be calling the shots. You hear me, Van? I'll be calling 'em like I see 'em. And I will thank you for giving me my start. I wouldn'ta got there without you. It's johns like you that'll make me a star.

VAN: No woman. We already got our piece.

LEILA: You never got a piece of nothing, you nappy island chimp!

She tries to hit him once again. This time he grabs her.

VAN: Nobody want you.

LEILA: You smell like your damn sorry island.

He kisses her hard and ugly. She spits in his face. He throws her to the floor.

VAN: One last look? All right then. Get up. Let me see ya on yer knees. Come on! Be real black for me. *(gyrating above her)* Show me what you got, woman! Let me see how black you really are! *(staggers away)* All right. I guess you got the job.

She lies still. Then slowly she rises. Something terribly changed in her.

LEILA: I give up. I'll give it up to you. Why don't you take it?

VAN: I don't want it.

LEILA: You been wanting me since before you was born. So take it, man.

VAN: Don't prostitute yerself.

LEILA: There's no charge. You ain't got no money anyway. You done pawned the club. Give it all away, you're whole damn life. So come on. Take me down with you. *(VAN turns away)* Take it! You tore me down, I'll be damned if you're just gonna walk away now. Vantyle, --

Tenderly, he touches her.

VAN: T'ink you hit it big. But not really. Not the way we look. Lower the ass, lessen the lips, lighten the skin. Wear fine clothes, wear rags. No difference. You can't escape yerself. Leila, --

They fall into an awkward, hungry, sad, loving kiss. As they embrace, Van begins to weep. It grows intense.

LEILA: Hey....Don't cry, baby....Don't cry.... *(sings)* DRY YOUR EYES//LET'S BE SWEETHEARTS AGAIN *(laughs through tears)* I'm the one who should be crying. I have nowhere to go

Van pulls away. Wipes away tears, fixes his suit.

VAN: I have to go. For good. I hit the bigtime, woman. Hit it on the nose. Brown Bomber couldn't hit it any harder.

LEILA: You won?

VAN: I put it all on the line. Every damn t'ing I got. Everybody else's money too.

LEILA: Then why you got the blues?

VAN: Blues? Nah! I got to skip town. But I want people to know I hit. That somebody can hit. I mean a nigger got to hit sometime.

LEILA: Then stay.

VAN: You tell them. Please. I'll pay you.

LEILA: *(knocks wallet from his hand)* I don't want your money, --

VAN: Then I'll pay you with a lesson King Joe taught me. Tonight I put it all together. Just me and the radio and the Joe Louis Blues. Backwoods Joe. We can't win, Woman. Not here, not now. But don't quit. Too many of we quit. Too many of we can't take the pain. This ain't how to hit. Big bets and half-ass blues. Songs can't swing hard enough. Try to hit, end up getting hit. *(kisses her hand)* But you. Know yer strength. We all go down. You tell me what make a King.

Van exits. Leila sees the wallet, picks it up, about to go after him. Opens the wallet. It is empty. Something about it all makes her smile. She sings the Joe Louis Blues, her way.

LEILA: LORD I HATE TO SEE// OL' JOE LOUIS STARE DOWN// LORD I HATE TO SEE //OL' JOE LOUIS STARE DOWN//BUT I BET A MILLION DOLLARS//NO MAN WILL EVER WEAR HIS CROWN

LEILA: BULLFROG TOL' BOLWEEVIL//JOE'S DONE QUIT THE RING// BULLFROG TOL' BOLWEEVIL//JOE'S DONE QUIT THE RIING// BOLWEEVIL SAY HE AIN'T GONE//AND HE'S STILL THE KING

As she sings the last line, we see JOE LOUIS in all his righteous glory, punching, the perfect champion forever etched in memory.

END OF PLAY

RAGGED TIME

CHARACTERS:

Blind Gary
Ignacio (played by a woman)
Freda
Abe the Newsboy
Blind Ross
The White Shadow
The Yellow Kid (played by a woman)
The Sanctimonious Kid (played by a woman)

TIME:
1898

PLACE:
A DEEP SOUTH OF THE MIND

So here I am, so here I am
Fake mammy to God's mistakes.
And that's the beauty part,
I mean, ain't that the beauty part.
    -- Robert Hayden, from
      "Aunt Jemima of the Ocean Waves"

RAGGED TIME was developed at the Royal Court, London, the Mark Taper Forum New Work Festival, and The Actors Studio West. It was premiered at The Black Dahlia Theatre, Los Angeles in 2002, directed by Matt Shakman; in 2007 The LAByrinth Theatre Intensive, NYC developed the revised and current version, directed by Marlene Forte.

The play is previously published in the anthology *Out of the Fringe: Contemporary Latina/o Theatre & Performance* (TCG Publications, 2000).

Time: 1898. Place: A Deep South of the Mind.

A crunched view of Charleston, South Carolina. Harbor, waves splashing against the Battery, antebellum villas. Aromas of Catfish Row and the syncopations of the red-light district.

Three realities simultaneously (marked with *):

*) WHITE SHADOW sits in a rocking chair. A Winchester rifle resting on his lap. BLIND ROSS plays guitar.

WHITE SHADOW*:* Play me a song. In the old style.

ROSS*: (Sings):* SOME FOLKS CALL ABOLITION// TRY TO MEND THE NIGGER CONDITION//I SAY LEAVE US BABIES ALONE

WHITE SHADOW: Niggers will always have a home.

*) IGNACIO plays ragtime on an upright piano. FREDA stands in her red-lit doorway. Her face heavily powdered.

FREDA: Can't ya play no white music? If this ain't whore luck I don't know what is.

*) ABE enters:

ABE: Papers! Get yer papers!!!*(no takers)* I love papers. Got yer front page! Got yer funny pages in the back. And in between -- well ya got yer adverts there! A triple-decker sandwich for the mind! Even if you can't read, ESPECIALLY if you can't. 'Cause they're fulla PICTURES!!! What a product! It's a can't-miss!!!*(scratching himself)* So what's wrong with these Southern jigs? Up North they sell like hotcakes. Down here I can't sell a stack to save my life. *(to US)* Buy a paper!!

FREDA: (to IGNACIO) And QUIT THAT NIGGER MUSIC!!! *(IGNACIO stops)* Kids give me the uglies.

From OFF, we hear a guitar blues. Piedmont style, with a heavy African rhythm. Then BLIND GARY enters, singing.

GARY: *(sings)* IT WAS A TIME WHEN I WENT BLIND//IT WAS A TIME WHEN I WENT BLIND//WAS THE DARKEST DAY I EVER SEEN//IT WAS THE TIME WHEN I WENT BLIND *(sniffs the air)* Smell a town. Sure you right. Funky town. Try to pretty it up with sugar and spice, but it's funk all right. Down 'neath the petticoats. *(strides)* This is my town.

He steps in a ditch and falls hard on his ass.

ABE*: (as GARY falls)* Criminy. *(helps him up)*Buy a paper, Jim.

GARY: What town is this?

ABE: I hate a daytime drunk. What you s'posed to do at night if you're drunk by day? Drink?

GARY: I wish I was drunk.

ABE: You punch-drunk?

GARY: I'm blind!

ABE: Blind? Ha! That's a good one.

GARY: Can't see a damn thing.

ABE: Where's yer boy?

GARY: Don't got one.

ABE: Whoever heard of a blind man without a boy?! You need a boy to lead ya!

GARY: To hell with boys. I'm a man.

ABE: A blind man.

GARY: It's a free country.

ABE: You said it. But even I know a blind man without a lead boy is up shits creek without a paddle.

GARY: *(sniffs)* It's Charleston, ain't it. Charleston sho nuff. Smell the funk.

Abe sniffs the air cluelessly.

GARY: Done reached Slavetown.

ABE: You say something, Winkie?

GARY: Glad to be home.

ABE: This is home? My condolences. We got real towns where I come from. I'm a Yank.

GARY*: (meaning the opposite)* I'da never guessed.

ABE: Pride of New London, Connecticut. Home of the World's Greatest Newsboy.

GARY: "Boy" --?

ABE: Sure. (*GARY snorts*)What of it?

GARY: Jew?

ABE: Yeah.

GARY: What the hell's a Jew doing down here?

ABE: I'm trying to sell papers!

GARY: Some newsboy.

ABE: Some blind man. Kinda surly for a darkie.

GARY: Kinda stupid for a Hebe.

ABE: What'd you call me?

GARY: Stupid?

ABE: Why I oughta --

GARY: You wouldn't hit a blind man.

ABE: You wouldn't see it if I did.

Backing away from Abe, Gary trips and falls hard.

ABE: Ha! Walk just like an Irishman! Ain't ya got no cane or nothing?

GARY*: (spits)* Kids took it.

ABE: Kids are like that.

GARY: I hate kids.

ABE: Guess that's why you ain't got no lead boy. Up where I come from we got dogs to lead the purblind.

GARY: To hell with dogs.

ABE: Buy a paper? Just a joke.

Gary removes a coin, takes paper, stuffs it in his vest.

ABE: I'm not sure if that's what Mister Hearst had in mind.

GARY: Cold coming on. Where the blackfolk hang out?

ABE: See that tree limb....?

GARY: Aw, to hell with you.

ABE: I found me a good dosshouse down East Bay Street.

GARY: Say what?

ABE: Doss -- Hotel de Gink. Wanna kip with me?

GARY: Just show me which way the whores is.

ABE: The whores?

GARY: Point me in the general direction, I'll be fine once I catch the scent.

ABE: I thought you blind streetsingers was supposed to have the gospel in ya.

GARY: Who says I don't? Whores got souls. So do blind mens. I'm just following God's will. I'll get to Zion some way.

ABE: Zion? I think you mighta taken the wrong turn somewhere.

GARY: You know about as much as a pig knows about napkins.

Then Ignacio resumes the ragtime. Gary listens, smiles.

FREDA: *(grumbling to IGNACIO)* You're getting on my last nerve....

GARY: *(suddenly walking confidently)* I'm fine. Fine as wine.

ABE: Sure you can't see?

GARY: This is my town.

Gary sniffs, walks towards the music. Abe watches him go.

ABE: *(smells the air)* Can't smell a durn thing. *(closes his eyes)* Just think, Kid. If you had to see through yer nose. But what if you had to sneeze? *(opens eyes)* Papers! Get yer papers from the World's Famous Newsboy!

Abe walks off. Gary approaches. Listens to the music.

GARY: Hands are small. Gal? Nah. See how he's always rushing ahead of the tune? Boy sho nuff. And not just any little bastid. That kid was born to ply.

FREDA: *(to IGNACIO)* I'm no mom, kid. Comprende?

IGNACIO: *(slight accent)* I get you.

FREDA: I felt bad for ya. Orphaned stowaway crying in the rain out by the Navy docks. Christian decency got the better of me. But you're getting on my last nerve! *(Ignacio stops playing)* Good! Now what do they call you? Ig-something?

IGNACIO: Ignacio.

FREDA: Yeah, Ignatz. Look. Kids is bad for business. So when I'm entertaining, it's out the door with you. Okee-dokee? This'll work out fine. *(Ignacio starts to play again)* If I don't kill you first.

Gary bumps into something close by. Freda hears it.

FREDA: Damn! I got a date, kid. Shoo!

She grabs him by the scruff of the neck and shoves him out the door.

FREDA: Skiddoo!

Ignacio bumps into Gary. Runs off. Freda applies powder to her face, then calls out:

FREDA: Come hither --! *(she sees his blackness)* Hmmph! You're a bold one.

GARY: Lovely perfume may I say.

FREDA: You may not.

GARY: Deelightful piana you ply.

FREDA: I don't play.

GARY: Then your son --

FREDA: Son? Ha!

GARY: My apologies. Your brother.

FREDA: That boy ain't mine.

GARY: You don't say?

FREDA: Just some little bastid Messican boy who followed me home last night. *(uncomfortable)* Why you stare at me like that?

GARY: It's just you look good enough to eat.

FREDA: You wanna get your head broke?

GARY: Long as I can lay it on your pillow.

FREDA: You are a sexy old buck. *(looks around, no one watching)* There's laws, you know. But it's been a slow day. Got money?

GARY: Right here in my pocket.

FREDA: Well come in then....And hurry up.

Gary stumbles on the threshold.

FREDA: What's wrong -- Ugh! -- You're blind!

GARY: *(grabbing her)* Yeah, but that never stopped me none.

FREDA: *(pushing him out)* I got my standards! Black AND Blind? What would people think?

GARY: Believe me, I'm quite developed in my other senses --

FREDA: Get off me, ya damn coon!

GARY: You sure are one uppity geechee tarbaby!

FREDA: Oh!!!

GARY: You better be fine and yellow 'cause your mouth is mighty bad for business!

FREDA: *(checking her makeup)* Sir. You are under a misconception!

GARY: Don't give me that. I smelt you a quarter mile off. Don't be bashful, honey. It's a respeckable trade for a brownskin gal --

FREDA: Am NOT!!

GARY: You mean you ain't a whore?

FREDA: OH!!!!

GARY: Or you ain't bla -- *(he stops)* Uh-oh. Put my foot in it this time.

FREDA: How DARE you.

GARY: *(checking his nose)* Never been wrong before.

FREDA: *(applying more powder)* I've never been so insulted!

GARY: You oughta get out more.

FREDA: You could get strung up for less.

GARY: Well I am blind...!

FREDA: Guess you couldn't help yourself.

GARY: A thousand apologies, all lined up with Valentines.

FREDA: Well all right then, but watch it now.

Ignacio sneaks back in to the piano.

GARY: But seriously, just between us folks -- Ain't ya got at least a smidgeon of the good stuff --? Brown betty? Hot fudge and raisins --? *(FREDA growls)* Okay, okay, I gotcha --!

FREDA: Not black!! You hear me?!!

Ignacio begins to play.

FREDA: IGNATZ!! QUIT THAT JIG PIANO!!

Ignacio stops.

GARY: That boy is music to my ears.

Gary reaches for something inside his sock.

FREDA: What do you think you're doing?

He pulls out his surprisingly large billfold.

FREDA: I said I won't take your business.

GARY: Not you. The boy.

FREDA: What do you want the boy for? *(crosses herself)* Don't tell me.

GARY: Be my pleasure to take him off your hands.

FREDA: Pervert! You one of them kind.

GARY: I could show you what kinda man I am. But if'n you won't let me, then let's us do some business.

FREDA: I'm a Christian woman.

GARY: Sure you right! *(pounding out the gospel)* GIMME THAT OLD TIME RELIGION//GIMME THAT OLD TIME RELIGION *(conspiratorial)* Kid'll be solid gone. Hard cash, babe.

FREDA: *(eyeing the billfold)* How much?

GARY: *(counting them off)* Squoze the nickel till the buffalo roared, and the eagle cried mercy.

FREDA: Someone like to roll you, blind man carrying all that cash alone --

GARY: Not alone. Not no more.

He places the bills in her hand.

FREDA: Oh, Ignatz --?

Freda pushes him Gary's way.

FREDA: Go on now. Go on with the nice man.

Gary feels Ignacio like a piece of bread.

GARY: I do believe I have been hoodwinked.

FREDA: *(counting cash)* Now what are you going on about?

GARY: This boy never worked a day in his life! Shoulders like a bird! This kid ain't nothing! Ain't ya got no other kids? I'll trade ya. You can have this one back.

FREDA: We made a deal.

GARY: This is bad business. What if I wanted my money back?

FREDA: I'd scream rape and the men of Charleston would string you up and set fire to your raggedy ass.

GARY: *(clears throat)* Well, in that case, I'll take the boy.

Gary throws his sack at Ignacio -- it is heavy.

GARY: You drop that, your ass is grass!

Gary pushes Ignacio ahead. Then Gary stops.

GARY: One thing. This here boy -- he's dark, ain't he?

FREDA: Excuse me?

GARY: Dark. Of skin. 'Cause Messicans is dark peoples, that's the way I remember anyways. If he's gonna be my lead boy, then he's gotta be dark. 'Cause we don't want no trouble.

FREDA: *(lying)* No trouble.

GARY: Then it's all right?

FREDA: It's made in the shade.

GARY: Then there's no trouble. *(cuffs IGNACIO)* Snap to it, you little so-an-so!

FREDA: It's Ignatz.

GARY: What kinda fool name is that? Ignatz ain't gonna win no favors.

FREDA: Look how much he's won already.

GARY: *(to IGNACIO)* You so much as think of running and I'll skin you alive and roast the rest for Sunday dinner.

IGNACIO: *(to FREDA)* MAMA --!!

GARY: I'm yer mama now.

They exit together. Freda pockets the cash.

FREDA: See how far you get beating on a white boy. Dirty mangy dog! *(beat)* Ah well. Kids ain't your style, gal. Hell, if you got a kid, then a husband can't be far behind....

Abe reappears in the distance.

ABE: Get yer papers! Don't nobody read the papers in this town?

*) Shift to the rocking chair. Ross plays masterfully.

WHITE SHADOW: Just like the old days.

ROSS: Just like 'em.

WHITE SHADOW: This new generation ain't worth shucks. Don't know their history. And they sure as sheepshit don't know where they're headed!

) DARKNESS. Or better yet, blindness. Gary's voice on the wind:

GARY: Lemme tell ya about blind mens. Don't never try to fight a blind man. We may not got eyes, but we gots some unnatural big hands, and when we gets to fighting, we let it all hang out. So if you value your life, say yassuh and do exactly as I say. *(beat)* And one thing. Don't ever...ever... even try to steal one of my songs.

Gary has a hold of the boy's shoulder. They are out of sync. Gary cuffs him.

GARY: Too fast! *(cuffs him)* Too slow! Move yer damn feet!

IGNACIO: Mama!

GARY: I'll mama you! I'll mom and pop you!!!

Ignacio flees. Hides behind a tree.

GARY: Think you can run back home? Miss Lady sold you for a song. This is home. *(beat)* I got my rights. I put my money down.

Stalemate. Gary has an idea. He removes the newspaper from his vest and sets it down on the ground. Then he lies back.

GARY: You'll come back. I got all the time in the world! Catch me some beauty sleep, forty winks do sound good!

Gary sleeps, or seems to. Soon he's snoring loud. The wind rustles the paper. A flash of bright color -- the funny pages. SOUNDS of manual typewriters, printing presses, freight train whistles. The tune "Yankee Doodle" played fast. All this coming a long way on the wind. Ignacio approaches stealthily. Disembodied VOICES egg the boy on.

VOICES: *(cartoony)* Have a look! Go on!

Ignacio grabs the funny pages. Immediate SPOT UP on THE YELLOW KID and THE SANCTIMONIOUS KID in primary colors as if from a cartoon. Their style is broad vaudeville.

YELLOW: If it ain't the Sanctimonious Kid!

SANCTIMONIOUS: The Yellow Kid. Fancy meeting you!

IGNACIO: Who are you?

YELLOW: We just told ya! Can't ya read? We're what's funny in the funny pages!

SANCTIMONIOUS: Haven't you ever heard of yellow journalism? We got a special way of burrowing into young minds.

YELLOW: We was drawn that way.

SANCTIMONIOUS: But that's another story.

Each extends a hand to shake. Each tricks Ignacio.

YELLOW: Go whistle!

SANCTIMONIOUS: This urchin is straight outa vaudeville! Falls for everything!

YELLOW: All the flim-flam.

SANCTIMONIOUS: All the phonus balonus.

YELLOW: The bunco schemes of the bunco steerers.

Sanctimonious tweaks Gary's ear. He reacts, swats at a fly.

SANCTIMONIOUS: Like the monkey's uncle here. We're the best friends you're likely to ever have.

YELLOW: We'll take a shine to ya. Seeing as you're so bug-ugly and pitiful.

SANCTIMONIOUS: Real Mama's boy.

YELLOW: Except he don't got a Mom! *(to SANCTIMONIOUS)* So whatdya say?

SANCTIMONIOUS: I say we get started. *(stares at IGNACIO)* So get started!

Ignacio reads the funny pages as they act it out:

YELLOW: How about a little burley-Q --?

SANCTIMONIOUS: A bit of Ethiopian minstrelsy --?

YELLOW: Coonshows?

SANCTIMONIOUS: Yankee Doodle played fast. We're out for fun and must have it. Let's get to work!

They fall into a series of pratfalls and somersaults, like a pair of old pros. They are just about to get into their gag, when --

Gary grabs Ignacio's wrist.

IGNACIO: Ow!

GARY: Kids and cartoons. Just like flypaper.

Wrestles Ignacio down, sits on him.

GARY: Ain't no kid gonna get the better of me. Never again.

GARY puts a dog chain and collar on Ignacio. The Kids watch.

SANCTIMONIOUS: I thought Lincoln freed the slaves.

) Ross spit-shines White Shadow's shoes.

WHITE SHADOW: Slaves? We loved 'em. Just like puppies. Just like little flop-eared puppies.

) Abe is also reading the funnies. The Kids approach him.

ABE: Heh-heh. Funny.

SANCTIMONIOUS*: (to YELLOW, at ABE)* What a rube.

Freda appears again at her doorway. Abe sniffs the air in imitation of Gary. Then he sees her.

ABE: Wow! What a looker! What a mink!

YELLOW: Cheese it!

SANCTIMONIOUS: This is rich.

YELLOW*: (whistles at FREDA)* Whistlebait!

SANCTIMONIOUS: The newsie is a mamaphiliac.

YELLOW: Gee, his Ma must be pretty old by now.

SANCTIMONIOUS: Pshaw, my foolish friend! A tit man!

YELLOW: Well she's sure got a pair!

ABE: *(to FREDA)* Hiya Kid.

Abe tips his hat. Freda double-takes at his appearance. The Kids crack up.

YELLOW: Duh!

SANCTIMONIOUS: The mater's rendered speechless.

YELLOW: He got a face that cud stop a clock.

FREDA: *(to ABE)* Are you all right?

ABE: This is how I look all the time. I been called the homeliest man in three states, but I can kid with the best of them. The name is Abe the Newsboy.

FREDA: Did somebody hit you?

ABE: *(a BELL rings)* Somebody?!! I had a thousand fights. How many you had? You're looking at the Middleweight Champ of New England, known in betting circles as the Connecticut Tiger. Gee, I like to fight. Fighting is like wine to me. They are wrong who think a Jew won't fight. I'm what you Southerners call a "Fighting Po' Fool" -- I get carried away with patriotism. I feel romantic towards women, I can see the old stars and stripes waving in fronta my eyes when I'm in ring center and the old fists are going sock, sock, sock -- so yeah, I been hit a few times. *(sniffs the air)* May I compliment you on your lovely perfume.

FREDA: What is it about my perfume today?

ABE: You must draw men like flies.

FREDA: I guess that's a compliment.

ABE: Say, if I didn't know better I'd say you was a Jew too.

FREDA: This is not my day.

ABE: Jews are beautiful people. Lucky no. But beautiful. People say Jews is lucky, but if every Jew was lucky there wouldn't be poverty with the Jews. And no Russian pogroms!

FREDA: Russian what?

ABE: Dontcha read the papers? Here.

He gives her one. The Kids cackle.

ABE: On the house. Don't say I never gave you nothing.

FREDA: A paper?

ABE: Greatest invention since outdoor turlets.

FREDA: Usually where I read 'em.

They accidentally on purpose touch hands.

YELLOW: Wouldn't it be funny if they --?

SANCTIMONIOUS: You mean, kisses at twilight --?

YELLOW: Moons in June and all that guff --

SANCTIMONIOUS: And nine months later --

YELLOW: Puke and screams!!

SANCTIMONIOUS: Pee-filled diapers!!

YELLOW: Poop in the bathtub!!

SANCTIMONIOUS: And no nooky to be had. Not with a kid around.

YELLOW: Wouldn't it be a laugh?

SANCTIMONIOUS: Would the kid look like him or her?

YELLOW: Would she sell it?

SANCTIMONIOUS: She did last time.

YELLOW: Selling kids is good business.

SANCTIMONIOUS: Especially if you're selling yourself and no one's buying!

YELLOW: Say, maybe I oughter sell you.

SANCTIMONIOUS: Long as it's paper money.

They crack themselves up.

FREDA: Why do you let them call ya "boy"?

ABE: What's wrong with boys?

FREDA: I prefer men. I steer clear of kids -- you end up a slave to them.

ABE: Don't talk to me about slaves! I left that stuff behind in Russia. Hey, every time a Russian has a problem, he socks a Jew for luck. But here, no matter who you are you're free. You're in Americker! This place beats all!

SANCTIMONIOUS: This fellow's got more gags than we do.

FREDA: Took too many punches, Yank.

ABE: 'Cause I love my country? Go on. You smokes oughta learn --

FREDA: *(overlapping)* Hey!

ABE: *(overlapping)* -- something from us Jews. You darkies oughta --

FREDA: HEY!!

ABE: -- be wiser than a buncha Bohunks and Russkies. Heck, you was born here, in good old Dixieland, under The Flag That Makes You Free!!

The Kids melt in fits of laughter. Freda laughs bitterly.

ABE: Go on and laugh.

YELLOW: Ikey!

SANCTIMONIOUS: Ikey Finkelstein!!

ABE: Go on. Show yer ignorance.

FREDA: "The Flag That Makes You Free?"

ABE: Go on. Give it the deep six.

FREDA: You're in the South, little man. You're in Charleston! Home of the whipping post, the auction block. The fine buildings? The pretty harbor? Where do you think the cash came from? You never heard of the cargo of Charleston Bay?

ABE: You never heard of the Cossacks?

FREDA: You're about thirty cents away from having a quarter, boy.

ABE: I just don't understand you shines --

FREDA: And don't NEVER say them words to me!

ABE: Which?

FREDA: *(applying powder)* I am a lady, if you haven't noticed.

ABE: I noticed.

Beat. They look each other over.

FREDA: I've a good mind to go back inside.

ABE: No! Please, Miss. I forget how to talk to a lady. Guess I got my bell rung one too many times at that.

FREDA: Is your face always like that?

ABE: They say when I'm asleep I look just like an angel.

The Kids watch them disgustedly.

YELLOW: Mushy stuff.

SANCTIMONIOUS: Let's get outa here!

They see the papers. They wink at each other. Each Kid takes an armful.

YELLOW: Sometimes you just gotta sell yerself!

They disappear.

FREDA: Jews. I know all about Jews. Worked a whorehouse next door to a synagogue. "Psst. **Kumt arien.**" Chains of whores. If you wanted one, the fancy dan would say sure, dollar for a colored, dollar fifty for a white girl. But a jewess was a bargain, only a dollar twenty-five. *(beat)* I knew a Jewess once, with a big belly. Fella would come, she'd ask "you wanna marry? I marry you. I make money." The dan would come in and slug her in the mouth. "When he comes to fuck you, you fuck him. Don't tell no stories about marrying, you sonofabitch, you lousy whore, you." But she never stopped asking. *(she* *holds his hand*) Didn't mean to bring ya down, Yankee Doodle. Yankee doodle doo.

They are about to kiss.

ABE: Hey, you wanna paper?

She shows him the one he already gave her. Abe notices that his stack has been pilfered.

ABE: Well I'll be rogered!

FREDA: *(takes his hand)* **Kumt arien**, Tiger.

She takes him inside.

*) Blind Ross plays for White Shadow.

ROSS: *(sings)* NIGGER'S HAIR AM VERY SHORT//WHITE FOLKS HAIR AM LONGER//WHITE FOLKS DEY SMELL VERY STRONG//NIGGERS DEY SMELL STRONGER

WHITE SHADOW: Now dance.

Blind Ross does a shuck an' jive, complete with waving arms and shit-eating grin. At the finale, Ross sticks out his hand for a coin. White Shadow, chuckling, drops one into his palm.

WHITE SHADOW: I like the way you do business. *(pats his head)* You my boy.

Winchester over his shoulder, he ambles off.

ROSS: *(flips him off)* You sure the fuck ain't my boy. *(bites on the coin)* Gots one song for the whitefolk to see, but the real song belongs to me. *(sings for himself)* I WILL DO MY LAST SINGING IN THIS LAND SOMEWHERE,....

As he makes his own blind way off into the shadows, --

*) Gary and Ignacio, now leashed to a dog collar he wears.

GARY: *(pulls the chain)* Time to earn your keep.

It starts to rain.

GARY: Well ain't this a blivit. Five pounds of shit in a three pound bag. Damn, I hate the rain.

IGNACIO: It's just the sky is crying.

GARY: What are you, a poet too? Up shits creek with a little Messican oarsman.

IGNACIO: Whoresman?

GARY: Naw, that's me.

They reach a busy streetcorner. Gary pulls the chain. They stand together. Gary gives Ignacio a tin cup.

GARY: Now look pitiful.

Ignacio holds the cup out, while Gary plays, pitifully.

GARY (sings) MOTHER AND FATHER BOTH GONE//MOTHER AND FATHER BOTH GONE//AIN'T NOBODY'S DARLING//NOBODY DON'T CARE FOR ME.... *(hissing)* I said pitiful!!!

CLINK. A single coin jangles in the cup.

IGNACIO: Gracias --

Gary kicks him.

GARY: Much obliged.

IGNACIO: Moch obliged.

GARY: *(retrieving the coin)* One penny. We'll go hungry for sure. *(to the boy)* Ain't there nothing you can do? Little shuck and jive? Little harmony? *(snorts)* 'Course not! Now hold that damn cup out there and look pitiful! *(IGNACIO tries)* That ain't it! *(Gary grabs Ignacio's face and makes a mask of it)* There. Don't move.

Gary starts to play. A lot more lively.

GARY: We gotta make something happen here. *(sings)* OH MY SOUL IS A WITNESS FOR MY LORD//MY SOUL IS A WITNESS FOR MY LORD//WHAT'S THAT RUMBLING UNNER THE GROUND//MUST BE THE DEVIL TURNING AROUND//WHAT'S THAT RUMBLING IN THE SKY//MUST BE JEHOVAH PASSING BY//DOWN CAME THE CHARIOT WITH THE WHEELS OF FIRE// TOOK OL ELIJAH HIGHER AND HIGHER//NOW ELIJAH WAS A WITNESS --

Ignacio starts to sing. It just pours out.

IGNACIO: FOR MY LORD

GARY: *(stunned)* ELIJAH WAS A WITNESS

IGNACIO: FOR MY LORD

GARY: ELIJAH WAS A WITNESS

IGNACIO: FOR MY LORD

GARY: YES ELIJAH WAS A WITNESS

IGNACIO: FOR MY LORD

Ignacio dances, a delightful innocent shuck and jive.

GARY: NOW DANIEL WAS A HEBREW CHILD//WENT TO PRAY WITH GOD FOR AWHILE//KING AT ONCE SAW DANIEL DESCEND//CAST HIM INTO THE LION'S DEN

IGNACIO: *(stopping on a dime)* THE LORD SENT AN ANGEL//THE LION FOR TO KEEP//AND DANIEL LAY DOWN//AND WENT TO SLEEP

(long pause)

GARY: DANIEL WAS A WITNESS

IGNACIO: FOR MY LORD

GARY: YES DANIEL WAS A WITNESS

IGNACIO: FOR MY LORD

GARY: NOW DANIEL WAS A WITNESS

IGNACIO: FOR MY LORD

GARY: YES DANIEL WAS A WITNESS

IGNACIO: FOR MY LORD

GARY: NOW WHO'LL BE A WITNESS

IGNACIO: FOR MY LORD

GARY: WHO'LL BE A WITNESS

IGNACIO: FOR MY LORD

GARY: WHO'LL BE A WITNESS

IGNACIO: FOR MY LORD

GARY: *(climaxing)* WHO WILL BE A WITNESS

IGNACIO: *(outclimaxing him)* FOR MY LORD

Coins pour in. The SOUND of a shower of silver.

IGNACIO: Much obliged! Much obliged!

GARY: Hoo baby! The eagle shits today! Where the hell did that come from? Don't answer, sing another quick. You know "Rock of Ages?" "Get on Board Li'l Chillun?" *(no response)* "Ezekiel Saw De Wheel?" "Joshua Fit De Battle --?" Boyo, you blowing our chances here.... *(plays and sings)* JOSHUA FIT DE BATTLE OB JERICHO//OH YEAH, OH -- *(IGNACIO is silent)* That's just fine! Hold out on me. Think you some kind of artiste? Too good for the shuck and jive? Listen. This aint art. It's business. Give the bucra what they want. *(takes the cup back)* You ain't gonna get my goat. I done fine without you. I don't need you.

(IGNACIO cries)

GARY: And quit sniveling!!

They sit in the rain. On the wind, Ignacio hears his RAGTIME.

IGNACIO: I miss....

GARY: Who? Your mama?

IGNACIO: *(plays the air)* I miss....The piano.

GARY: That's what's wrong with pianos. Can't cart them out in the rain. That's why God made these babies. *(strokes his guitar)*

IGNACIO: But I don't play guitar.

GARY: Well maybe you gotta learn to play piano on the guitar.

The music wafts away. Only the sound of rain.

GARY: Damn this rain! Newspaper sticks to ya!

Gary violently pulls the newspaper from his vest, throws it onto the street. Ignacio picks them up. As he reads:

YELLOW: Hook, line and sinker!

SANCTIMONIOUS: Let's break the kid in easy.

YELLOW: Or just break him.

"Yankee Doodle" played fast. A cartoon backdrop appears, a fence with a hole in it and a sign which says "BEWARE OF EVERYTHING, ESPECIALLY THE DOG" -- vaudeville stuff. Like two old vaudevillians, the Kids bow.

YELLOW: *(taking center stage, spelling out a newspaper title)* THE YELLOW KID LOSES SOME OF HIS YELLOW! *(runs to fence, acting out the cartoon)* Here comes that other kid. I'll just hide. *(stands at the hole)* Boy he'll be surprised to see me standing here.

Sanctimonious approaches. Then something pulls Yellow from behind. His face contorts. Sanctimonious laughs.

YELLOW: *(responding to the tug)* Somebody has took unfair adwantage of me! *(another tug)* I'm behind in my rent or vice versa!

Sanctimonious helps pull him away from the fence. A dog -- TIGE -- who looks suspiciously like Abe, has the backside of Yellow's smock in his jaws.

TIGE: Yow!

YELLOW: Hully Gee.

SANCTIMONIOUS: Good dog, Tige.

TIGE: Arf!

Yellow turns his back, exposing his torn backside to us. "Yankee Doodle" and a laugh track as the Kids bow. But Ignacio does not laugh. The Kids frown at him.

SANCTIMONIOUS: Harummph!

YELLOW: How come he don't like the funnies?

SANCTIMONIOUS: How should I know?!!

YELLOW: No respect for art. Whatdya want? the Mona Lisa?

SANCTIMONIOUS: Maybe it's you.

YELLOW: ME?!!

SANCTIMONIOUS: Maybe his tastes are a little more... how shall I say...sophisticated?

YELLOW*: (turning up his nose)* You mean soup-an-fishticated?

SANCTIMONIOUS: Swellegant!

YELLOW: So the spic is a swell! Rat bastid.

Ignacio keeps reading. More "Yankee Doodle" and vaudeville.

SANCTIMONIOUS: I'm on!

YELLOW: Break a leg! for starters....

SANCTIMONIOUS*: (spells out his newpaper title)* THE SACTIMONIOUS KID JUST PRACTICES ON HIS VIOLIN!

Sanctimonious produces a violin and saws upon it. Cats shriek and smoke emits from the prop. Tige appears.

TIGE: Yow Yow.

SANCTIMONIOUS: Tige, I've an idea to get rich quick, but you must help me.

TIGE: I'm with you, Buster.

Sanctimonious and Tige put on dark glasses. Sanctimonious plays violin while Tige holds out a sign which says "WE ARE BLIND." They ape Gary and Ignacio. Coins pour in.

BOTH: Much obliged! Much obliged!

Then a COP WHISTLE.

YELLOW: Cheese it, the cops!

Mad scatter.

SANCTIMONIOUS: *(pointing at TIGE)* Run! This dog is mad!!

Tige froths at the mouth. Backdrop flies off. Then Tige and Sanctimonious come together to count the change.

SANCTIMONIOUS: Resolved! That there is money in music and with money one can be kind and generous and good! Here, boy! *(gives TIGE his cut)*

TIGE: Thanks, Kid.

SANCTIMONIOUS: Blindness pays in aces!

YELLOW: Aw feed it to the fish!

"Yankee Doodle" along with bows and laugh track. But Ignacio is stone-faced.

SANCTIMONIOUS: Gee. Nary a titter.

YELLOW: Tough nut to crack. *(inspects IGNACIO)* Kid thinks he's some pumpkins.

Ignacio begins to hum the RAGTIME.

*) Abe and Freda in bed together.

ABE: *(awakens from a dream)* **Mommychen hilf mier!**

FREDA: **Nummdich zusammen.**

ABE: Where the heck am I?

FREDA: How soon they forget.

ABE: *(flexes muscles)* I'm a new man.

FREDA: I'm the same woman.

ABE: I dreamt I was in my mama's arms. But youse a lot darker than Mom. Prettier too -- sorry Ma! -- mit hips. Oh mommy, what a dream! We was way out on the deep water, come halfway across the world with the Cossacks giving chase, and now at the very mouth of Lady Liberty, the freight goes and sinks on us! But God Bless the U.S. Navy. Picked us right outa the briny and brought us into port. All pea-coats and bell-bottoms and brass buttons. That's when I figured out, this is a pretty swell country.

FREDA: I see the Navy a little different.

ABE: *(oblivious)* That's why I'm heading down to Cuba.

FREDA: You going to war?

ABE: Sure, seeing as it's all about liberty and freedom and such. We're gonna liberate them Cubans from the shackles of Spanish slavery.

Abe rises -- he's wearing a red union suit.

ABE: If the papers say go, I'm going! The papers gave me my education. My kid's gonna learn the same way.

FREDA: Your kid?

ABE: I love kids.

FREDA: Don't they give you the uglies?

ABE: No more than usual. *(off her reaction)* Whatsa matta, babe?

FREDA: Just wondering why you're talking about KIDS!

ABE: It is kinda funny at that. You'd think we was getting married or something! *(laughs uneasily)* You'd think.

FREDA: That's a laugh.

ABE: Yeah, a real hoot. *(watches her dress)* When I woke up and saw ya, I swear I thought I was in heaven. You was Faith, Hope and Charity all rolled up in one hot little package!

FREDA: You got the charity part right.

ABE: Checked my wallet, did ya? You don't know where I keep my secret riches --

FREDA: *(holds his cash)* You mean this? *(he snatches it back)* You got about enough to buy a cup of coffee.

ABE: Times is tough.

FREDA: I thought you Yanks was supposed to be rich. Now I feel like offering you a loan. But how about I let you have a free one instead.

ABE: I don't accept charity.

FREDA: Me neither. I prefer handsome men, but with you I'll make an exception. If you play your cards right.

ABE: I don't like cards. I like fighting.

FREDA: I swear I don't know what I see in ya.

ABE: It's the muscles. Gals go for 'em.

FREDA: *(plays with his ears)* Nope. It's the ears.

ABE: But they're two cauliflowers!

FREDA: They do look like flowers, kinda.

They make out a little. Then he looks her in the eye.

ABE: I'm confused here. Help me out. You took to me like a Jewess, but you looks like a Negress. What does that make you, some kinda Mulatress?

FREDA: Down these parts there's a lotta mud in the water. But that kinda talk can hurt business.

ABE: Whose business?

FREDA: MY business! I'm the kinda gal who wants to go top-dollar. So I put my best foot forward.

ABE: Which foot?

FREDA: Being black gets awful inconvenient.

ABE: Ta hell with color. I say give it up. One woman's the same as another.

FREDA: *(angering fast)* Who do you think you're talking to?

ABE: I'm telling you something. I meet all kinds in my business.

FREDA: So do I.

ABE: What you get all outa joint about? I never saw you before and you never saw me before.

FREDA: I never saw you before and I never want to see you again!

She storms out.

ABE: *(shouting after her)* I don't give a hoot what color you are! *(to himself)* What a woman. *(dresses quickly)* I'll look for ya later!

FREDA: *(from OFF)* Fat chance!!

ABE: *(out the door)* I'm in love!

Abe walks onto the street. Sees Gary slumped like a dead man.

ABE: Hey Winkie! Guess you didn't find your scented pillows, after all.

GARY: *(sniffs the air)* Guess you did.

ABE: I got lucky, I sure did.

Abe sees Ignacio. Tucks him under the chin.

ABE: Guess you got lucky too! Pretty little gal you got there... Yessirree... Hey, wait a -- this is -- It's a boy!!! I thought you was a regular guy, not one of them Greek types!

GARY: Don't worry, Newsdummy. He's my new lead boy. *(cuffs IGNACIO for show)* Mind yerself.

ABE: *(to IGNACIO)* Ow! You don't gotta take that!

GARY: Yes he do.

ABE: What are you? Some kinda communist? One of them Black Russians?

GARY: I'm always rushing one way or the other. But simmer down. This here's my son.

ABE: Your son?!! *(breaks out laughing)*

GARY: What?!!

ABE: Don't you know? This child is WHITE! He is a member of the White Race, once you dust him off a little.

GARY: But the kid's a Messican --!!

ABE: A Greaser? He's toasted awful light if you know what I mean.

GARY: But Messicans is dark! And I bought me a Messican!

ABE: You been sold a bill of goods.

GARY: *(faltering)* Bad business. How white is he?

Abe rubs Ignacio's cheek, smudges it pink.

ABE: Not near dark enough for you.

GARY: She said Messican....

ABE: Don't take it so hard. Just looks kinda funny. White kid leading a smoke.

GARY: Backwoods Bucra would skin me alive, once they finished laughing.

Gary approaches Ignacio, without malice.

GARY: Well Kid. This is it. I thought deep down we was the same. So that, bad as I was, you'd see I was still better than the white man. I can't figure it out. You got the music like I do. Whitefolk just don't smell the same, you know? *(sniffs the air)* Damned if you still don't fool me. I gotta give you up, Kid. Coulda taught you things, not the shuck an' jive, but the stuff from the other side, from our people over there -- *(gestures beyond the bay)* Our father's fathers. But I gotta let you go.

Ignacio kneels in the mud. Puts mud on his face.

GARY: What you doing? What you up to?

ABE: Hey! Whatdya know? The kid he's browning himself right up!!

GARY: What?

ABE: He's putting on the blackface for ya! Well if that don't beat it!

GARY: Jesus, Kid. You know what you're doing?

IGNACIO: I'm playing the piano...on the guitar.

Gary embraces him.

ABE: Why you wanna go with him? Hell, if you go with him, why not go with me? Yeah! Why not? I can teach ya how to box! I'll take ya to Cuba with me!

GARY: Hey wait a --

ABE: Shake hands with Abe the Newsboy! Hero of a Thousand Fights!

GARY: Now looka here --

Abe shoves him aside.

ABE: The papers, they could be your future!

Gary shoves his way back to Ignacio.

GARY: Let's get outa here, boy.

ABE: Offer stands, Kid.

Gary grabs Ignacio's arm. Abe grabs Ignacio by the other arm. It seems they might tear the boy in half. Ignacio, saving himself, slips out of his coat. Without him in it, both Gary and Abe lose their balance and fall on their asses. Ignacio looks from one to the other. Then he picks Gary up. They exit fast. As they do, they nearly run into White Shadow, Winchester under his arm. Gary, smelling him, backs off fast.

GARY: Excuse me, Mister White Man, suh!

White Shadow watches them go. Abe scratches himself.

ABE: Aw what the hey. What's a kid if you ain't got a wife? Sheez. *(to WHITE SHADOW)* Buy a paper?

White Shadow takes a paper from the stack.

WHITE SHADOW: WAR WITH CUBA? *(flips ABE a coin)* The War ain't in Cuba, my friend. The Real War is right here. Down home.

White Shadow tips his hat, walks on.

ABE: I don't like the cut of his jib. *(examines the coin)* You just sold yer first paper in Charleston, kid! *(beat)* How come it feels so cold?

) Out of town, a country road. Train tracks, the sea close by. Hunter's moon on the rise. Gary and Ignacio walk. Ignacio holds the papers in his hand.

GARY: Whatchu doing? Reading them funny papers? Can you read? What the front page say?

IGNACIO*: (reads headlines)* WAR WITH CUBA.

GARY: Hrmph. We always got to pick a fight with somebody. What else it say?

IGNACIO: AMERICA DEFENDS HONOR OF RAVISHED CUBAN WOMANHOOD.

GARY: That's a laugh. America ain't doin' nuthin but defending its own interests! As always!

IGNACIO: NAVY DOCKS IN CHARLESTON HARBOR -- NEXT STOP HAVANA.

GARY: Hope they take the Newsbozo with 'em. Ain't ya got no other news?

IGNACIO: SEA SERPENT SWALLOWS BATHER IN EAST RIVER.

GARY: Now that's more like it!

IGNACIO: SPARSELY CLAD BEAUTIES FROM POLYNESIA.

Takes the paper away from Ignacio. Tucks it in his vest.

GARY: We'll read that later. Lemme tell ya something, boy. This a damn rag. And I don't mean no ragtime. Oh it's fun. But it don't sing and it don't ply. *(sings and plays)* IT WAS A TIME WHEN I WENT BLIND//IT WAS A TIME WHEN I WENT BLIND//WHEN I LOST MY SIGHT, I HAD A LOT OF FRIENDS//LORD THEY TURNED THEIR BACK ON ME,.... *(as he plays)* Ain't no paper can do dat.

IGNACIO: Can I?

Offers to take Gary's guitar. Gary slaps his hand away.

GARY: Think I'm stupid? Try to steal my songs. Try to rob me blind.

IGNACIO: You blind for real?

GARY: Unfortunately, yeah. Brick to the side of the head. But it take more than pain to stop this dark horse. Hell with them!

IGNACIO: Who?

GARY: Kids! Since then I see everybody the way they looked as kids. *(suddenly lashes out)* Go on! Leave me be!

Ignacio HUMS his ragtime. Then Gary sniffs the air.

GARY: Well I'll be goddamned....

Enter BLIND ROSS. Sniffing. Gary and Ross face off like two big mangy dogs.

ROSS: Blind Gary.

GARY: Blind Ross.

Each spits.

GARY: Nice to see ya.

ROSS: Nice to be seen. Long time.

GARY: Not near long enough.

Ross sniffs the air, towards Ignacio.

ROSS: Son?

GARY: *(a hiss to IGNACIO)* Watch yerself!

Ross offers the boy his guitar.

ROSS: Hold this fer me, will ya? When I catch my breath, we'll share some songs. What's mine is yours. 'Course, knowing Gary, you prob'ly know all my songs by now, seeing as he done pilfered alla mine.

Ross sits down like he's home.

ROSS: Gonna be a cold night. What say we make us a fire? Just like old times, Gary. Like when you was my lead boy. *(big grin)* Wanna ply?

Ignacio looks to Ross, then to Gary. Ignacio's hand hovers over the guitar strings. As Ross laughs, --

END ACT ONE

ACT TWO

In darkness:

GARY: Dark, ain't it. Maybe a flash here. Streak of blood there. Now try moving. Kinda clumsy, huh? *(beat)* Just think. Always this. Always wondering about the next step. Unless you can find a way to see. And once you got that seeing thing, you ain't wanna lose it.

*) Campfire near the train tracks. Ross plays and sings. Ignacio soaks it in. Gary sits apart, deathly still.

ROSS: *(singing and playing)* I DON'T KNOW WHERE I WILL BE//SINCE MY GOOD CHILD WILL BE LEADING ME --

GARY: Like hell.

ROSS: I WILL PAY MY LAST VISIT IN THIS LAND SOMEWHERE....Sing it with me, Gary Boy.

GARY: Ross, you kill me.

ROSS: Wish I had me a boy.

GARY: You had many a boy.

ROSS: *(to IGNACIO)* Gary and me, we come to Charleston onct, many years ago.

GARY: You was a slave in Charleston.

ROSS: Gotta let that slave stuff go. I went down to the Old Slave Mart this morning. Strange to walk there free as I please. Don't nobody spit no more when you brush shoulders on the street. I even got a coin or two. And the smell.... *(sniffs the air)* Not that old slave smell. Not like in our time, eh Gary? Now they got a bakery right there by the auction block. Right there where they used to sell our mamas and our papas in the noonday sun.... *(plays instead of speaks)* Smell of baked bread instead.

GARY: Funk's there. It don't fool me.

ROSS: Come here, boy. Lemme show you how.

Ross gives his guitar to Ignacio, who picks out his ragtime. Ross laughs like the Buddha. Gary growls, turns away.

*) Abe, trying to hawk papers to no success whatsoever.

ABE: *(to AUDIENCE)* Come on! Be a man! Buy a paper! *(no response)* Don't be shy. We're Americans, we ain't a shy people! We see injustice, we set it right! Don't we? This ain't just paper! This is our country here!

Freda promenades in, dressed to the nines.

ABE: Wow.

FREDA: If it ain't the news butch. Long time no see.

ABE: T'ought you didn't want to see me.

FREDA: That was hours ago. So how's tricks?

ABE: *(scratching himself)* Business is up.

FREDA: *(adjusts a stocking)* Up all over.

ABE: *(scratching)* Nothing like a war.

FREDA: I walk down Broad Street, I lost count how many men of Charleston come looking to plant their little American flags in me. Like I'm Cuba! And all I wanted was a cup of sugar. I'm baking a cake. Wanna piece?

ABE: Cakes are for kids.

FREDA: Well you call yerself a boy. *(he keeps scratching)* Got fleas? Take a bath in sand and a rubdown in alcohol. Fleas'll get drunk and kill each other throwing rocks.

ABE: No fleas.

FREDA: Good, 'cause then I'd have 'em.

ABE: I gotta sell these papers.

FREDA: Why are we talking about paper? when you can have your cake and eat it too? Angel food. My special recipe....

ABE: Devil's food was good enough last time.

FREDA: Why do you insult me to my face? Have the decency to do it behind my back like everybody else in this godforsaken town. I don't look -- *(can't say the word)* I mean my features aren't Afri-- .... And my pigment, I've worked very hard on my pigment! I've put good money down for the best Parisian face wash --

ABE: They got stuff for jigs?

FREDA: On second thought, no cake.

ABE: Look, sometimes I don't say what I mean. I like you. And heck! With them voluptuous features of yours, you could be anything!

FREDA: Anything but American.

ABE: American as me!

FREDA: Ain't saying much, Abe Hollandersky.

ABE: I'm pretty voluptuous myself. We're equals!

FREDA: Equally lousy.

ABE: I told ya, no lice! I been doused!

Abe shows Freda his scalp. Freda takes the paper.

FREDA: You don't think this is lousy? *(reads from it)* CUBAN MONKEYS -- Are Cubans really monkeys?

ABE: Monkeychasers, maybe.

FREDA: *(reading more)* DARK-SKINNED DEVILS....

ABE: I don't write 'em, I just sell 'em!

FREDA: Feed folks the same damn mistakes --!

ABE: Mistakes? What mistakes!

FREDA: Mistaking me for a darkie!!!

ABE: What do the papers gotta do with that?

FREDA: Everything!! It's all in black and white! Everything's black and white!!

ABE: There's color supplements on Sundays --

FREDA: You miss what's in between!

ABE: I didn't miss you.

FREDA: No, you got what you wanted.

ABE: Well, I guess, but ....

She starts crying.

ABE: Well if this don't take the rag off the bush! How come you're crying--?

FREDA: You don't care!

ABE: I do too care.

FREDA: You talk nice now, but you want to plant your flag in me same as the next guy!

ABE: Well, yeah, but -- NO!!

FREDA: You judge me.

ABE: Babe, take a hard look. Who am I to judge? I'm a Jew pug been hit more than the Liberty Bell. And the papers? You saw my finances. I can't even give 'em away. The South is killing me! The only reason I haven't shipped out of here is, well, I hoped we might see each other -- and not like that! I mean for a walk, arm and arm-like and the whole shebang. My steamer left a couple hours ago. Jacksonville, then Cuba. And now you're here.

FREDA: Am I your Cuba?

ABE: You're my All-American gal.

They embrace.

FREDA: Liar.

ABE: Life seems pretty black and white to me. But maybe that's why you stand out.

FREDA: Like a sore thumb.

ABE: Like a lady. But you oughta settle down. You got a mighty fine head on your shoulders, and I don't much care what color it is.

They kiss. Sanctimonious and Yellow pop up.

YELLOW: I hate this gooey stuff.

SANCTIMONIOUS: Funny how a person can go and sell a child, then turn around and kiss and hug like nothing happened.

YELLOW: People is funny.

SANCTIMONIOUS: Hylarious!

YELLOW: We could give him a hot-foot. Tie his shoes together --?

SANCTIMONIOUS: Too easy. But we can't go empty-handed, now can we?

YELLOW: Let's swipe his precious newswipe!

SANCTIMONIOUS: We already did once.

YELLOW: But you can never have enough toilet paper!!!

They make paper airplanes and other projectiles. By now Abe and Freda have retired to her bedroom, and are in the midst of undressing. Both are shy, tentative.

FREDA: You married?

ABE: Nah. You?

FREDA: You kidding?

ABE: What do you think about kids?

FREDA: Kids?

ABE: So you want one or what?

FREDA: Do you?

ABE: Sure t'ing!

FREDA: Oh.

ABE: You mean you don't?

FREDA: Messes with the figure.

ABE: What if ya didn't start from scratch? If there happened to be one readymade? I saw this kid who just about fits the bill. Aw he's a great kid.

FREDA: Was he ...? Was he ...with somebody?

ABE: He was leading some blind spook -- I-I mean spade -- I-I mean --

FREDA: Black bastid!!

ABE: That's the ticket! Kid's a pip! Maybe I should find him, bring him to ya ....

She vigorously shakes her head no.

ABE: Whatsa matta? Look a little green about the gills. Can't be that bad. Lemme guess. Is he yours?

FREDA: Hell no!!! I mean -- *(struggling)* He was given me .... I mean he was -- I was -- It was just business!!!

ABE: Kids are great for business!

FREDA: Abe, it wasn't like that.

ABE: You don't gotta apologize, I'm looking for free help myself --

FREDA: The blind fella took --! he took --!

ABE: The boy!

FREDA: Well not quite.

ABE: I wasn't born yesterday! You got tooken! And so did the kid!! Why, if I were from these parts, I'd lynch him -- but I'm not. There was bad business here, and I've an idea to set it right.

FREDA: How?

ABE: Well, they got a headstart. But then again, we got eyes. *(throws on clothes)* We're gonna free the kid!!

FREDA" What if the old buck don't want him freed?

ABE: He'll listen to reason.

FREDA: *(fingering her billfold)* But what if we have to pay?

ABE: Who'd sell a kid for cash? Even he couldn't be that much of an animal! *(FREDA squirms)* Get your clothes on.

FREDA: Why dontcha just give him one good shot behind the ear?

ABE: We're gonna play this fair and square. Hell, even if we do gotta pay him a coupla bucks so he don't go away mad.

FREDA: You don't got a coupla bucks.

ABE: I know.

FREDA: All right, all right .... *(pulls out her large wad)* It's not as much as it looks. Most is spoken for. Bizness expenses, the cops. *(off his react)* You got to pay, one way or the other.

ABE: You ain't doing that no more.

FREDA: It's my business.

ABE: Not no more. You and me are going into business together.

FREDA: What kinda business?

ABE: The Family Business! *(hugs her)* We better shake a leg! We'll find the blind fella. We'll reason with him. And if he don't wanna give the kid up, then we'll reason some more. And if still don't say uncle, well .... *(makes a fist)* He won't know what hit him.

As he swats the air, --

*) *The campfire. Ross sings and plays, Ignacio in his lap. Gary staggers off, still growling.*

ROSS: *(sings)* I WILL DO MY LAST SINGING IN THIS LAND SOMEWHERE ....

IGNACIO: Did you get used to being blind?

ROSS: You learn to see other ways. Me, I was born blind. Big, strong, happy, and blind. *(plays the guitar)* When you' blind, it's a wild bust of color. The way it looks, the way it busts and dances and jumps and fools around, almost like a buncha crazy kids in your head. Just like a buncha kids. When you're blind, you can see it better.

Ross motions for IGNACIO to sit on his lap.

IGNACIO: Do I have to go blind?

ROSS: You don't gotta do nothing you don't wanna do. *(ROSS kisses IGNACIO)* Now Uncle Ross he's a little different from Uncle Gary. Ross got faith in the little things in life. The road's a lonely place, and Gary he don't know nothing but womens. But Ross been on the road a long time. Ross been many a boy's companion on a cold dark night when the wind is blowing hard and ain't nobody else give a damn if you lives or dies. But Ross gives with all his heart. So you can come with me .... *(IGNACIO struggles)* Ross needs ya more than Gary ....

GARY*: (sniffing)* Boy!

Ignacio tries to rise, but Ross holds him down.

ROSS*: (whispering fast)* You and me, we cut out towards Distant Island, Gary don't know that place, --

GARY: *(approaching)* BOY!!!

ROSS*:* And I don't hit! Never hit a soul in my life. Come on!

GARY: *(finds them)* Shoulda known.

ROSS: Easy now Gary boy --

GARY: I ain't yer boy no more!

ROSS: *(to IGNACIO)* He was onct. Didn't buy him or steal him. Gary come of his own accord.

GARY: You know what this fella's all about, don't ya boy --?

ROSS: Gary was my boy. Back then Gary had eyes. But mostly he had eyes for my songs. Always looking at my hands. I could feel it. You robbed me blind. I could rip that lying tongue out yer throat!!

GARY: BULLPIZZLE!!!

ROSS: HOGPOOP!!!

Suddenly they are swinging at each other, missing wildly. Part melee, part ballet, both men tough as all hell.

GARY: So I stole! I'd do it again!!

ROSS: Aintcha learned nothing?!!

GARY: Them bucra kids took my eyes 'cause I plyed too good!

ROSS: Them bucra took yer eyes 'cause you was showing off to they womenfolk! You couldn't see the danger you was in.

GARY: I seen my own blood. You can't see a damn thing, Ross.

ROSS: I could see you wasn't taking care of business, fool!

GARY*: (so angry he's crying)* Business! That's all you ever cared about! Sure I stole yer songs. You never gave me nothing! I caught a whupping for any damn thing! Just for the fun of it! Just for the show! *(weeps)* I shoulda run off a thousand times!!!

ROSS: I didn't make ya blind, Gary. All I did was teach you how to ply.

GARY: When that brick hit me upside the head, and the Devil's own hellions laughed while I went blind....The whole time you kept on plying the guitar like nothing happened. Just kept on singing and crying. *(beat)* That was the time that I went blind.

ROSS: You got to let things go.

IGNACIO: Boss!

Ignacio goes to him. Gary pushes him away.

ROSS: Well Boy. Who you gonna turn to?

Abe and Freda enter.

ABE: Hi Folks! *(to FREDA)* That's him, ain't it? I got lousy night vision.

GARY: When it rains it pours.

Abe offers his hand for Ross to shake. Ignacio sees Freda.

FREDA: Hello there...son.

IGNACIO: Moch obliged.

ABE: Hey Kid.

FREDA: We come to bring you home.

Ignacio bolts. Abe ends up with nothing but the boy's coat. Ignacio runs full-speed into the Kids.

YELLOW: Say!

SANCTIMONIOUS: Going somewhere?

IGNACIO: Let go!!

*) They take Ignacio up into an as-yet undisclosed TREEHOUSE full of swiped papers, projectiles, toys, grafitti. A turn-of-century kid's paradise.

*) Down below, --

ABE: Where'd he go?

ROSS: I din't see nothing.

ABE: Is blindness catching?

*) Ignacio plays with a slingshot.

SANCTIMONIOUS: Careful there, you'll put out an eye.

IGNACIO: What happened?

SANCTIMONIOUS: You climbed a tree.

IGNACIO: I did?

YELLOW: Well you're up one now.

SANCTIMONIOUS: Let the kid have a look at what he left behind.

*) *They look down.*

FREDA: You said you'd get him!

ABE: I will, babe.

FREDA*: (glancing uneasily at GARY)* Do it quick.

SANCTIMONIOUS: Go back down if you want to.

IGNACIO: I don't want to.

SANCTIMONIOUS: Suit yourself.

YELLOW: Nah, let's us suit him!

*) *Yellow puts a cartoony sombrero on Ignacio.*

IGNACIO: What's that for?

SANCTIMONIOUS: Dontcha wanna be like us?

YELLOW: We don't take guff from nobody!

SANCTIMONIOUS: Except for Mister Hearst.

YELLOW: Except for Hearstie.

SANCTIMONIOUS: We don't like the way these so-called adults keep playing ya like a poker chip! You're a kid by gosh by gum, and you're not gonna take it anymore! No one can push us around!

YELLOW: Except the Hearstmonster.

SANCTIMONIOUS: But I don't see anyone remotely like Bill Hearst around here? Do you?

YELLOW: Just a coupla mashiated blind guys and an overgrown newsbaby.

SANCTIMONIOUS: Not to mention the lady. The lovely lady who sold you in the first place.

YELLOW: Without even offering you a percentage!

SANCTIMONIOUS: The nerve!

YELLOW: You been taken unfair adwantage of! But we're here for ya!

SANCTIMONIOUS: It's a little like this Cuban War. There wouldn't be a war if it weren't for our beloved Boss Hearst.

YELLOW: *(reading a headline)* HOW DO YOU LIKE THE JOURNAL'S WAR?!!

SANCTIMONIOUS: We started a war. Just think! A pound of toilet paper with a raving lunatic's ink smears, and out comes the U.S. Navy no less to do Boss Hearst's bidding and crush the aforementioned enemy, whoever they may be! So we figured, what the hey! If a newspaper can start a World War, then why can't a pair of fine upstanding Kid Celebrities --

YELLOW: That means us!

SANCTIMONIOUS: Why can't we come to the aid of a poor little Messican bastid orphaned in the jungle camps of the Deep South? Why can't we take a moment out of our busy schedules to take History by the scruff of the neck and give her a good swift kick in the slats, for a friend in need?

YELLOW: So here we is!

SANCTIMONIOUS: We'll show ya the power of paper. You need us, and by gosh by gum we need you too.

IGNACIO: For what?

YELLOW: For Business!!

SANCTIMONIOUS: We're on a promotional tour. Hearst wrote us a *carte blanche*!

The Kids produce an oversized cheque.

YELLOW: Don't it make your mouth water?

SANCTIMONIOUS: Leave it go, you'll smudge it!

They gesture towards the piles of kid stuff.

SANCTIMONIOUS: We got all this merchandize!

YELLOW: Try this on for size!

SANCTIMONIOUS: No charge!

YELLOW: Hold him down!

They overpower Ignacio and force him to dress up as a cartoon character -- specifically a cartoon Mexican. They have all the paraphernalia -- poncho, cigar, fake moustache, ukelele. Ignacio ends up a cartoon kid, part Keaton, part Cantinflas, with a Pierrot-like melancholia.

SANCTIMONIOUS: *(introducing)* Ladies and Gentlemen ... The Lost Boy!

YELLOW: Still bug-ugly. Who's gonna laugh at him?

SANCTIMONIOUS: He may lack our particular genius for comedy, but there's something innately ridiculous about his very being that tends to make the common man chuckle.

YELLOW: You mean 'cause he's a spic?

SANCTIMONIOUS: The unwashed phenomenon. *(laughs)* It's fun to condescend. *(to IGNACIO)* Enjoy the world of two dimensions! The land where cause has no effect, or the other way around. Be a kid cartoon, go on! Give comedy a try!

YELLOW: The world is your erster!

SANCTIMONIOUS: Oyster.

YELLOW: Aw feed it to the fish!

"Yankee Doodle" played fast. The Kids looks to Ignacio.

SANCTIMONIOUS: *(stage whisper)* That's your cue.

YELLOW: Do something!

Ignacio picks up the uke. Plays the tune to his ragtime. Yellow sticks his fingers in his ears.

YELLOW: Whodya t'ink you are? Paganinny?

Ignacio plays the rag. Even on the uke it is beautiful.

SANCTIMONIOUS: Argggh! Don't ya see? That's what's holding you down!

YELLOW: That kinda music's too real! You'll never get free!

Ignacio loses himself in the ragtime, tears in his eyes.

SANCTIMONIOUS: Feeling? Feeling's just a great big leg iron. And music is a whipping post! We freed ya from all that! And what do you do? You sit there and stare at us with the shackle in your hand!

YELLOW: It's enough to gimme the blues.

SANCTIMONIOUS: And what do you do? You "ply" the uke!

YELLOW: Really gimme the blues.

SANCTIMONIOUS: Americans are happy! We like a joke! Even if it happens to be on us! We don't want blues! We want action! Thrills!

Ignacio starts to cry.

SANCTIMONIOUS: What is it with you people?!!

Ignacio is playing with a feeling and a soul not heard before on a ukelele. The Kids can't helping being affected, no matter how much they may fight the feeling.

YELLOW: Real laff riot.

SANCTIMONIOUS: *(huffy)* Oh great. Make us feel two- dimensional. You think we have no hearts? Well we don't! Cartoons aren't supposed to feel. It gums up the burleyque. *(almost pleading)* We're offering you an out from the infinite sadness of your life! I thought you said you didn't want to go back!

IGNACIO: I don't.

YELLOW: Then what the heck are ya doing?

SANCTIMONIOUS: Yeah! What are ya trying to be?

He stops playing. Wipes his eyes. Smiles.

IGNACIO: Free, I guess.

*) Below, Ross plays. Gary sniffs around near Freda. Abe and Freda searching fruitlessly.

ABE: Kiddio!

FREDA: C'mere pumpkin! *(under her breath)* Little bastid.

GARY: *(sniffs the air)* If it ain't the funkytown gal!

FREDA: Shhh!

ABE: Say something?

FREDA: Nothing snookums. Try over there ....

Abe ruts around out of earshot. Then to GARY:

FREDA: Keep it down.

GARY: We done bad business. You sold me the boy under false pretenses. You knew if I went backwoods with a white boy they would lynch me. You knew --

FREDA: Hoped, maybe.

GARY: I want my money back.

ABE: You say something?

FREDA: Nothing, snookie! *(to GARY)* For godsakes, quiet.

GARY: Well?

FREDA: Put out your hand.

She puts her wad of bills in his hand.

GARY: What's this?

FREDA: I don't wanna hear no squawking, you ol' rangtang. This is payment in full, *(this pains her)* with interest. Now gimme the kid.

GARY: Now you want the kid?

FREDA: I got a chance at something. And I don't wanna mess it up.

GARY: *(sniggering)* You want the kid!

ABE: Wha?

FREDA: Nothing, Puddin'! *(to GARY)* You got your money. So shush.

GARY: The Yank don't know you sold the kid?

FREDA: Please. Don't say nothing.

GARY: Why shouldn't I?

FREDA: 'Cause I'm asking. I'm asking ya nice. *(he keeps sniggering)* Don't refuse a lady.

GARY: You refused me.

FREDA: That was business!

GARY: And now it's more than business, in't it, Puddin'?

FREDA*: (despairing)* What do I got to give ya? *(GARY grins)* All right, all right.

Freda maneuvers him professionally behind a tree.

FREDA: Just try not to make any noise.

GARY: Little ol' me? *(to ABE)* HEY NEWSBABY!!

FREDA: Bastid!!

Abe approaches. Freda jumps away, applies makeup as fast as she can.

GARY: Whatcha up to, boy?

ABE: Well I'm looking for a kid about yea high.

GARY: Why in hell wouldya want to do that?

ABE: 'Cause I'm gonna be his pop. And she's gonna be his mom! *(GARY sniggers)* Don't snigger at the lady, there's a good scout, eh Jim?

GARY: Well Deacon, you'd snigger too if you saw what I'm seeing.

ABE: I got this lousy night vision.

FREDA: Dirty mangy dog.

GARY: Smell the air, Ross.

ROSS: I'm smelling it.

GARY: You know what it smell like.

ROSS: Sho nuff.

GARY: *(sniggers)* Smell like sex.

ROSS: And cabbage.

GARY: Say what?!!

ROSS: Cabbage, sho nuff.

GARY: Ross getting a little long in the tooth.

ABE: What say we quit the pleasantries. We're here on business.

FREDA: Abe --

ABE: I'll take care of this, babe. We want the kid and we're ready to offer you --

FREDA: Abe --!

ABE: Not now, babe! We're doing business.

GARY: Some business!

ABE: We're prepared to pay!

GARY: Kid's value done sky-rocketed! None of us can afford him!

ROSS: Much less find him.

ABE: He'll turn up.

GARY: If he does, he ain't for sale.

ABE: It's been my experience that most men can be bought.

Gary tosses Freda's money on the ground.

GARY: Not this time.

Freda snatches it up violently.

ABE: Is that yours?

FREDA: Just take the damn kid!

GARY: Over my dead body.

FREDA: That can be arranged.

ABE: No need threatening -- just yet.

FREDA: Abe, I swear! I'll tell you all about it, soon as we get home. (*seductive*) I promise. I'll make it all right.

GARY*: (sniggers)* So you're gonna Mom-and-Pop-it. Know what you're getting into, Newsboy?

ABE: Now the future missus and me, we got faith in God and Country and the Almighty Dollar, and we plan to pass that faith onto the boy. The papers made me what I am today. You watch what they do for the kid.

GARY: You think the papers, let alone God and Country, give a goddamn about you?

ABE: I do!

Gary removes the funny pages from his vest.

GARY: Ain't nothing but a rag! And here you want to stick that rag clear down to his soul and gag it for good! Raggedy ass --

FREDA: I wouldn't talk.

GARY: No, you oughtn't to. We all know what kinda business the lady runs.

FREDA: Watch it!

GARY: The Passing Business! Putting on a face, but it don't fool a dog like me. You can't lose the funk. I can almost taste the blackness --

FREDA: Bastid!!

Freda runs at him. Abe has to hold her back.

ABE: You really wanna call a spade a spade? You beat the boy. I seen ya.

GARY: What the hell do any of us know, but beating? Beat every damn day of our godforsaken lives! Eh Tigerman? What else we got but shame? Eh Slabberchops?

Gary suddenly swings at Freda, a near miss. Freda screams, then attacks. Abe can only barely hold her back.

FREDA: What I got to be ashamed about? I can't help it if I was born lucky!

ABE: Shouldn'ta taken a poke at a lady. You're lucky you're blind --

GARY: You think a blind man can't fight?

FREDA: Cream him!!!

ABE: Come on, now. Let's not be rash.

GARY: I'll raise a rash on yer ugly puss. You assified auntie-man! You lapdog! You Navy Boy! I'll knock ya piss-to-windward. I'll mash ya front to back!!

ABE: Talks a good show, don't he?

FREDA: All bark and no bite.

Gary punches Abe, hard.

ABE: Ow! Well whatdya know? He jooked me in the eye! If that don't beat it!

Gary punches again. This time Abe the professional eludes the blow, then wraps Gary in a half-nelson.

FREDA: MURDER HIM!!!

GARY: OW!!!!

ABE: This doesn't have to be like this, friend. Now. Apologize to the lady.

GARY: Never! *(ABE applies his trade)* OW!!! I'm sorry, dammit!

ABE: There's a good scout. *(looks at FREDA)* Now. You gonna sell us back the kid?

FREDA: Abe!

ABE: You sold the boy. Right?

GARY: *(still struggling)* Not as stooopid as you look!

ABE: *(applying more pressure)* I asked you a question.

GARY: To hell with -- *(ABE squeezes)* ARGGH!!

ABE: Think about it. Take your time. We got all the time in the world ....

GARY: Damn! I hate pain!

FREDA: Just kill the bastid and we'll keep the money.

Abe lets Gary go.

ROSS: No wonder the boy done gone.

FREDA: Shut your trap unless you want some of the same.

ABE: Quit volunteering me to fight old blind guys, okay? I'm a professional!

GARY: Professionals I'll say! Professional liars and sluts!!!

Freda hits Gary in the eye. Gary grabs his eyes. He shakes head to foot as if doused in cold water. He seems to be undergoing a change, some kind of revelatory moment.

GARY *(prophesying)* I see.

FREDA: You're blind!

GARY: I had to find a way to live. And knowing no different, I lived like a slave. I put that in the music. And I gave that music to the boy. I made him my slave. And you all would do the same, if you could.

FREDA: Speak for yourself!

ROSS: Young Lady, my folks was slaves. Your folks was slaves. All our folks was slaves. That's something we got in common. Then, by God, how's it come to pass that we become the slavers now?

ABE: Slavers?

FREDA: I ain't no slaver!

GARY: You just sell the meat.

FREDA: You bought it.

GARY: Indeed I did.

ABE: *(chastened)* I did too.

FREDA: Abie! Don't listen to these raggedy fools!

GARY: Ragged is the word. Ross, the very mention of your name makes me spit. But you done hit the nail on the head this time. Here we be, slaving with the best of 'em.

ROSS: I'da done it too. Tried to turn the boy's head, but not for him. For me.

GARY: Most dreadful day I ever did see. 'Cept it's a bit of laugh too.

ROSS: 'Cept it ain't really.

GARY: No it ain't. *(shouts at the sea)* Sail away, boy!! Sail the hell away from us!! BE FREE!!!!

FREDA: We'll find him. Right Abe?

ABE: Naw babe. It's late and I'm bone tired.

FREDA: You giving up on me?

ABE: No one should ever call Abe Hollandersky a slaver. My mom and pop would be sore ashamed.

FREDA: Abe!

ABE: Maybe it's all been a big mistake.

FREDA: I swear I'll never sell a kid again! I'll never sell a living soul!!

ABE: What about yerself?

FREDA: I'll give it up! I will. Starting right now I'm turning over a new leaf. *(ABE sighs heavily)* What.

ABE: Watch the ones who turn over new leafs. You tend to find the old one underneath. Sorry babe.

FREDA: Oh. So it's like that.

ABE: We musta been crazy. I'm keeping ya from yer business, and yer keeping me from mine. Hey. No hard feelings. Friends?

He offers his hand to shake. She bats it away.

FREDA: I don't got any friends. See ya down Charleston Bay. And don't you say a word unless you got your money ready.

) Above them, in the treehouse.

IGNACIO: They're sad.

SANCTIMONIOUS: My pitiful friend -- Some people are born sad, some achieve sadness, and some have sadness thrust upon them. In other words, who knows, --

YELLOW: And who cares!!

IGNACIO: I do.

YELLOW: There's yer problem!!

IGNACIO: My mama --

SANCTIMONIOUS: The one who left you high and dry?

IGNACIO: My papa --

YELLOW: The one who beat yer ma --?

IGNACIO: They came --

YELLOW: For a quick buck?

IGNACIO: For me. They came for me. They tried to give me --

SANCTIMONIOUS: Shitty pomes and nigger music --

IGNACIO: They tried to give me --

YELLOW: They gave you nothing!

IGNACIO: This one chance.

Ignacio plays the uke sadly. Then a string breaks. The Kids take it back from him.

SANCTIMONIOUS: These feelings? They'll pass. Like the measles and the mumps and poison ivy.

YELLOW: Like scabies! Hey, it's just one life, and a pretty lousy one at that!

SANCTIMONIOUS: Now envision this scenario. No parents, no history. No history, no memory. No memory, clean slate. Think of that -- a clean slate! That's what Boss Hearst sent us out to look for! You! You and the million other yous coming into Ellis Island and wading across the Rio Grande and getting born into the lovely tenements of the Lower East Side! Kid, you're the New American. You're gonna build our pyramids! You're gonna save your pennies, you're gonna make a buck or two here or there, and you're gonna spend 'em on the Funnies, or whatever technological equivalent thought up by the mind of Hearst, and all the other Hearsts to come. You, Kid, may be the Lost Boy, but You Have Been Found.

Ignacio removes his cartoon finery.

YELLOW: Hey. What the hey?

SANCTIMONIOUS: Be careful, that's a store model --

IGNACIO: Let me be free.

YELLOW: You can't escape us!

SANCTIMONIOUS: You belong to us --!

Sanctimonious puts a hand on Ignacio. Surprisingly, Ignacio pushes Sanctimonious and he falls in a big way.

YELLOW: Hully Gee.

Yellow does the same. Gets pushed, falls just as big.

SANCTIMONIOUS: What whatdya know?

YELLOW: Kid's got potential!

IGNACIO: I have history! Mama, Papa. Even if they never come back. I have them. I have them here. *(his heart)*

Ignacio begins to climb down.

SANCTIMONIOUS: Wait! If you go back, what do you go back to?

YELLOW: It ain't safe!

Ignacio shrugs. He takes the uke.

IGNACIO: I'll keep this.

YELLOW: Nuh-uh!

SANCTIMONIOUS: It's an original.

YELLOW: It ain't in stock.

SANCTIMONIOUS: Don't got all the kinks out yet.

YELLOW *(sad)* And besides .... It ain't real.

SANCTIMONIOUS *(sadder)* The real one's down there.

*Ignacio gives it back. Climbs down. Stays out of sight.

ROSS: It's an old story. My mother sung it to me, my mother's mother sung it, my grandmother's mother's grandmother sung it back in Bible days. And wouldn't you know, here we go again.

GARY: Just like the Children of Zion.

Abe and Freda stand apart, neither willing to exit first.

FREDA: Why aintcha pushed off yet?

ABE: Maybe I ain't so swift as you. Maybe I gotta think about my next step. *(to the blind men)* I feel like the Children of Zion too, ya know. I happen to be one!

FREDA: Aw, go sell a paper!

ABE: I don't care about papers. I'm talking about history.

FREDA: I thought papers was history.

ABE: This is history. You, me. Hell, we make our own history. No matter what happened in the past. This country is a our slate -- right now, right here --and we get to rub it clean. *(a fighting pose)* I'm the slate. And look at me now! Abe the Newsboy!

FREDA: *(with disdain)* Real clean.

ABE: I think so. I come a long way. And my kid is gonna come a long way further. And his kid. And all the way, till we finally get to Zion. That's what a kid can be to folks like us. *(tenderly)* You done a bad t'ing. I done bad t'ings too. But it's got to stop. It's got to stop! This is a free country!

FREDA: Nothing free. We both know that.

ABE: But one day it'll be.

Abe offers Freda his arm.

ABE: Lemme walk you back to town.

FREDA: All right, but you know you're not coming home with me --!

ABE: Heck no! I'm going to Cuba!

They start to go. Abe stumbles blindly.

FREDA: What's wrong?

ABE: It's awful black out there!

ROSS: Hey Jew Boy! You blind?

ABE: Right now I am!

ROSS: Well then God bless ya brother.

GARY: Never thought I'd call ya brother, brother!

FREDA: Come on, Kid.

ABE: You jigs -- I mean dar -- I-I mean -- Criminy! You fellas are okay by me!! *(to FREDA)* Come on, **pussil**.

FREDA: That sounds dirty ....

They start to exit into the night. Before they can go, White Shadow appears. Points the Winchester at them.

WHITE SHADOW: Hold on now. *(everyone freezes)* Ain't nobody going nowhere.

He looks them over. They all look down, subservient.

WHITE SHADOW: Treed ya. Just like treeing a runaway slave. You bring it all back home, chillun. I could feel something lawless, something wrong. But I am the law tonight. What kinda business ya'll up to? Blind men, whores, jews -- niggers? What kinda evil thing y'all up to? And where's the kid fit in? You devils gonna cook him up in a pot? Or is it White Slavery? *(off their react)* That's it. You gonna sell him!

GARY: Slave days over.

WHITE SHADOW: You think so? *(laughs)* You really think so?

ABE: No slaves in this country, friend.

Slings the rifle over his shoulder. Grins at Abe.

WHITE SHADOW: Don't believe what the papers say. Slavery won't ever die. Even you mudbabies figured out how good a business it can be. Maybe you call it something different now, but a rose by any other name smells just as much to high heaven.

He winks at Freda. Sniffs the air.

WHITE SHADOW: Nice perfume you got on. Too bad you had to go and sweat all over it.

FREDA*: (desperate)* The kid's gone!

WHITE SHADOW: Tell you what. Sell the kid to me. I'll bring him up to me a good little houseboy. Ply me a good ragged time and keep the bed warm on a cold night....

Gary hits White Shadow on the jaw.

White Shadow aims the rifle, but Abe knocks it aside. Abe hits White Shadow once more, with purpose. Then he stands above the prone body.

FREDA: Oh Abie. You gone and done it now.

GARY: He dead?

ABE: He'll come to, eventually.

But when he looks at his fist, he sees white powder on the knuckles.

ABE: What the hey?

Freda inspects his fist. Feels her own cheek.

FREDA: Some traditions go a long way back.

The Blind Men sniff the body.

GARY: Funky.

ROSS: Sho nuff.

FREDA: I may just have to get outa town. Better safe than sorry.

ABE: You can come with me. There's a steamer tomorrow morning. *(to the BLIND MEN)* You fellas gonna be all right?

GARY Don't you worry about us.

FREDA: Then we better git.

Abe and Freda exit. Gary and Ross are alone. Only the sound of the water lapping on shore.

GARY: Just me and you.

ROSS: And the boy.

GARY: Boy's long gone.

ROSS: Maybe.

Ross begins to pack up.

GARY: Where you headed?

ROSS: How the hell should I know?

GARY: Always wondered what I'd do, running into you after all these years. Split you down the middle with a broken bottle? Oh I had my dreams. But here we sit. Like nothing ever happened.

ROSS: Everything happened.

GARY: Thing is, Ross. I missed ya. Feeling ya around, near. Feeling ....

ROSS: Feeling.

Awkwardly, the two men touch hands. Not unlike the Sistine Chapel image. Then Gary clears his throat and starts to pack up his things.

GARY: Well if you find him somewheres, don't spoil him too much. I know you can't keep your hands off, but go easy. And let him watch ya good when you ply. Let him have it better than I did.

ROSS: And you.... If you happen to run into ...somebody....treat that somebody with a little warmth now, ya hear? Warmth. That's what a body's good for.

GARY: You talking about the nasty?

ROSS: Quite the opposite, quite the opposite. But you'll be nicer. Next time you'll be nicer.

GARY: Ross.

ROSS: Gary.

GARY: See ya around.

ROSS: In a manner of speaking.

Ross is gone. Gary is alone.

GARY: I could never be a mom or pop. You're lucky to be free of me, boy. Guess it's all for the best.

Breathes in deep. Then plays Ross's song:

GARY: Songs belong to everybody. *(sings)* I WILL DO MY LAST SINGING IN THIS

LAND SOMEWHERE//I WILL DO MY LAST SINGING IN THIS LAND
SOMEWHERE

Ignacio approaches the body of White Shadow.

GARY: I DON'T KNOW AND I CANNOT TELL WHERE//I MAY BE SOMEWHERE
SAILING IN THE AIR//I WILL DO MY LAST SINGING IN THIS LAND
SOMEWHERE ....

Ignacio covers White Shadow with the funny pages. Like a blanket, like a shroud.

GARY: I WILL TAKE MY LAST JOURNEY IN THIS LAND SOMEWHERE//I WILL
TAKE MY LAST JOURNEY IN THIS LAND SOMEWHERE ....

IGNACIO: *(sings)* I DON'T KNOW WHERE I WILL BE// I MAY BE OUT ON THE
OCEAN, WAY OUT ON THE SEA ....

BOTH: I WILL TAKE MY LAST JOURNEY IN THIS LAND SOMEWHERE!

GARY: You was up that tree. *(laughs)* Smelt ya all along.

Ignacio plays the guitar.

GARY: Whoa baby! Who taught you that?

IGNACIO: My people.

GARY: Messicans?

IGNACIO: Cuba.

GARY: You Cuban? Cuba libre!

They embrace.

*) *The Kids watch from above.*

SANCTIMONIOUS: Gee.

YELLOW: Another sucker bites the dust.

*) *As Gary and Ignacio go off together, --*

END OF PLAY

CONJUNTO

CHARACTERS

GENOVEVO, a Mexican adult man.
MIN, a Japanese-American adult man.
TED, Min's younger brother.
SHOKO, a Japanese-born adult woman.
PICHUKA, a Chicana woman in man's clothes.
ESQUINCLE, a Mexican adult man.
MACIAS, a young Mexican man.
SHERIFF/FBI MAN,/INS MAN, each or all a white man.

PLACE

Burbank, California, 1942-44, and the land of movie idols.

"Daichi" and "Conjunto" are songs written by Hisao Shinagawa.

CONJUNTO was developed at the Mark Taper Forum Latino Theatre Initiative, and The Sundance Theatre Lab. It premiered at Teatro Vision, San Jose in 2003, directed by Karen Amano. A revised version premiered at Borderlands Theatre, Tucson, AZ in 2006, directed by Armando Molina; and at Playwrights Arena, Los Angeles, directed by Jon Lawrence Rivera.

SCENE 1

BURBANK, CALIFORNIA, 1942. Spring.

In semi-dark, sounds of Spanish, Japanese, Filipino and English phrases exclaiming sleepiness, soreness, fatigue.

As the sun rises, --

GENOVEVO: **Vamos a trabajar!!!**

THE FIELD. A row of WORKERS dressed in overalls, hats, scarves and bandanas. Short handled hoe in hand, they move in synch not unlike a dance. They sing "DAICHI"—"The Earth"—a Japanese work chant.

WORKERS: **AIN-YA COLASHO//DOC-COISHO//NUNNO COLASHO//AIN-YA COLLASHO//BOC-COISHO//NUNNO-COLASHO....**

As they labor, --

ESQUINCLE breaks away. Throws down his hoe. GENOVEVO, the foreman, stands watching. So does MIN, the farm owner. A silent glance between them. Esquincle packs a carpet bag. Genovevo approaches.

GENOVEVO: Esquincle! Come back to work.

ESQUINCLE: **No mas!** Genovevo. **No mas! Pinches Yamadas!** They work us like slaves! On our hands and knees like hunchbacks, weeding, cutting, setting runners, irrigating—

GENOVEVO: Hell, that's just picking berries.

ESQUINCLE: It's that damn short hoe! A regular long-handled hoe would do just fine, but no! **Chapos cabrones!**

GENOVEVO: They don't want to bruise the plants.

ESQUINCLE: So they bruise us instead! **Me voy!**

GENOVEVO: You really think there's a place where things work better?

ESQUINCLE: Maybe heaven.

GENOVEVO: Or the movies.

ESQUINCLE: **Chale**! Moviestars got it even worse than we do! At least I don't gotta pretend how I feel.

GENOVEVO: How do you feel?

ESQUINCLE: Like I can't work for Japs no more.

GENOVEVO: Why, **Compadre**? Pearl Harbor got nothing to do with strawberries.

ESQUINCLE: I'm a pelado. Work my fingers to the bone for somebody else—**es la vida**. But this is 1942. I can't mess up my future! I gotta go.

GENOVEVO: Where?

ESQUINCLE: There's betas in Bakersfield. Garlic in Gilroy. The world is my oyster!!

GENOVEVO: I'll miss you. My **compadre**. Without you my Spanish will go all to hell. *(Genovevo gives him a bottle of tequila)* For the road. And when that's gone, lots and lots of menudo.

ESQUINCLE Why wait? **Salud**!

GENOVEVO: **Salud**!! May our dreams come true.

ESQUINCLE: **Cuidado** with your dreams.

They embrace. Esquincle exits into the sun. "DAICHI" grows in volume. Arnulfo breaks off.

ARNULFO: Can a fellow get a break around here? **Titi mo**. I got a hangover this big.

MIN: Take five.

They stop. ARNULFO, Filipino, drinks water. MIN YAMADA, the boss, drinks deep. Douses his head with water.

SHOKO: **Mottainai**!!

MIN: I'm not wasteful! I'm just hot.

SHOKO takes the ladle. Like a dog, Min shakes his head dry. Sprays Shoko with water.

SHOKO: **Bakabakashii**!

MIN: Don't talk Japanese. You know I don't understand that stuff.

SHOKO: You want me to translate?

MIN: No thanks.

ARNULFO *(grabbing his head)* Ugh!

MIN: Arnulfo had a few too many at the fights last night.

ARNULFO: He was a **Pilipino** like me! **Gagoo**! Lose every time.

MIN: Shoulda bet on the American guy! We win every time!

ARNULFO: Shoko, why you no come with us?

SHOKO: I don't like fights. I like movies.

ARNULFO: Who'd you see last night?

SHOKO: Gene Autry. He always wins.

MIN: I think she's sweet on him.

SHOKO: Ssshh!

TED, MIN's younger brother, suddenly lights up.

TED: You like Westerns 'cause it's like Old **Nippon**. You like them cowboys 'cause they're like samurai. Except they got better haircuts!

SHOKO: I just like them.

MIN: Back to work.

ARNULFO: Sure was a quick five.

Genovevo returns to the field.

MIN: Esquinkly's gone, is he?

GENOVEVO: Sorry Boss. He was my **compadre**.

ARNULFO: If he didn't quit, Boss was going to fire him. Always complaining, -- *(mimes drinking)* Always **weng-weng**. Lazy bastard, --

MIN: He didn't like to work? Or he didn't like to work for me? What's he think? I'm

Admiral Tojo? *(nervous laughter)* **Compadre,** huh? Maybe you think the same thing. You can go too.

GENOVEVO: Boss, no, I want to stay.

SHOKO: Mino-San! **No-moa!!**

MIN: No more what?

Shoko starts working alone. Ted joins her. Even Arnulfo.

MIN: I guess we're going back to work.

GENOVEVO: **Vamos.**

SHERIFF enters, tacks a notice nearby.

MIN: *(tips hat)* Howdy. *(no response)* Must be hard of hearing.

SHERIFF: I can hear ya fine. But it won't make a bit of difference.

Sheriff exits. The notice flaps in the wind.

MIN: *(to GENOVEVO)* Better get that before it blows away.

Genovevo retrieves the notice, brings it back to them.

SHOKO: What is it?

GENOVEVO: Relocation Order.

MIN: Here it comes.

ARNULFO: You guys are in trouble now.

As TED reads, FBI MAN appears from surveillance nest above. Patent leather shoes suit and tie. The voice of the notice.

FBI MAN: Aliens! Continue to work your crops until exclusion is ordered officially.

ARNULFO: Told ya.

FBI MAN watches, Edgar Bergin to Ted's Charlie McCarthy.

TED: "No crops should be destroyed. Federal officials are now being appointed to assist in the transfer of property—"

Min takes the paper.

MIN: Nobody gets this property.

SHOKO: **Mino-San**, --

MIN: We're Americans—*(nods at SHOKO)* Except you. We were born here! We didn't get brung up Japanese.

TED: We got brung up like a buncha monkeys.

MIN: That's the truth. *(crumples it up)* We're citizens.

SHOKO: It didn't say "citizens". It said "aliens".

MIN: And that ain't us. So don't worry. Heck, Ted and me, our draft status is 1-A! If this country is willing to send us to war, how can we be aliens? We'll be okay, Doll.

SHOKO: **Dame!** Don't say that.

MIN: What?

SHOKO: Don't say doll.

MIN: Okay babe.

SHOKO: **Dame!**

MIN: Shoke. All of you. This isn't war. It's a buncha **hakujin** sharpies looking at our berries and seeing dollar signs. Looking to scare us off. It's hardball. It's business.

SHOKO: Then I hate business.

MIN: Good. Leave the business to the men. Come on, we're wasting light!

GENOVEVO: **Vamos a trabajar! Rapido!! Vamonos**!!

They fall into line. FBI Man stands and watches.

FBI MAN: Any person who fails to comply will be subject to immediate internment.

As they sing "DAICHI"—

Scene 2

Twilight. Ted and Genovevo use concrete to fix a leak. Shoko uncrumples the notice.

TED: *(RE: the pipe)* This thing is pretty busted.

MIN: We'll fix it in the morning. *(Min pulls out whiskey)* Let's have a nip. So to speak!

TED: Not me.

MIN: *(as TED exits)* Good guy. Clean liver. Wish I could give him a little joy in his life. *(toasts GENOVEVO)* To Mexican girls. Hot **tamales**!

GENOVEVO: To hot **tamales**!

MIN: How come you don't got a Mexican girl?

GENOVEVO: I can't get married like this.

MIN: What's wrong with this?

GENOVEVO: I don't own anything!

MIN: Owning is a headache!

GENOVEVO: I dream of such headaches.

MIN: You wanna be like me? Get yourself a little **rancho**, eh?

GENOVEVO: Sounds like heaven. But it takes **lana**.

MIN: Lana? Lana Turner?

GENOVEVO: Cash money.

MIN: Hell, you got enough cash money, even Lana Turner would come along for the ride.

GENOVEVO: I'll settle for a nice Mexican girl.

Shoko listens in. Min lights a cigar.

MIN: Don't settle. Don't be like me. Everybody told me it was time to start a family and settle. So I settled. *(beat)* But you know me, like to buy the girls a drink. Do me a favor, Genovevo, buy lots of girls a lotta drinks. On me.

GENOVEVO: All I need is one—girl I mean. Land, and a good woman. My dream.

MIN: Me, I'd rather sing. And not that Japanese stuff neither. Gimme The Ink Spots and let her rip! *(sings)* I'LL GET BY, AS LONG AS I HAVE YOU!

GENOVEVO: You got a nice voice, Boss!

MIN: You oughta hear Ted. We could be the Oriental Ink Spots! We'd do it if I didn't have this farm around my neck—*(stops short)* Just a pipe dream anyway.

GENOVEVO: *(sings)* BUT WHAT CARE I?

MIN: SAY I'LL GET BY

BOTH: AS LONG AS I HAVE YOU!!!

Shoko stops listening.

MIN: You don't sing so bad yourself!

GENOVEVO: *(folds hands in namaste)* **Pues, arigato gozaimasu.**

MIN: **Puras papas**, you crazy Mex!

Genovevo about to exit when—

MIN: Do me a favor. *(beat)* Burn a piece of land.

GENOVEVO: I don't understand, --

MIN: I know the difference between words. Alien. I'm a citizen! Destroy my crops, as if I ever would, as if I ever could! How dare they? *(beat)* So burn just a bit, eh? I don't want to break the law. But I don't want the law to break me either. *(Genovevo amazed, nods)* And don't tell Shoko. These Japanese gals don't got no sense of humor!

GENOVEVO: **En bocas cerradas, no entran moscas.**

Genovevo exits.

MIN: Best foreman I ever had. *(swigs)* **Banzai!!**

Shoko combs out her hair. Min, drunk, enters the bedroom. Shoko holds his kimono. Min drops his pants, slips it on.

MIN: I'LL GET BY— *(winks)* Knock me a kiss.

Grabs her from behind and kisses her.

SHOKO: Your breath!

MIN: Just a couple cigars. Hey, have a drink with me! *(gets the cold shoulder)* You know, Kid, you can relax. My house is your house. We got the deed.

SHOKO: Do we? "Relocation" it said.

MIN: Yer killing my buzz!

SHOKO: "Internment" it said.

MIN: Nothing's gonna happen!

SHOKO: Why do you say that? Because you're afraid --?

MIN: Not afraid!

SHOKO: Or because you drank half a bottle of Crown Royal?

MIN: *(acting butch)* I'm the man. What I say is right. Japanese enough for ya?

SHOKO: No. Not enough.

They sit apart. She applies oils to her long hair.

MIN: Smells nice.

SHOKO: My hair? It's dry.

MIN: California dry. I do like it when it bakes. But then them Santa Ana winds come cool things off. And that marine layer comes and moistens the land and turns that dust back to soil and we can all live another day....and life ain't so bad. We just gotta get through the spring.

SHOKO: *(embraces him)* Mino-san. You are too headstrong.

MIN: But it's sexy, --

SHOKO: Too foolish, --

MIN: But don't it make you wanna snuggle?

SHOKO: *(breaks away)* **Yakimash-neh**! You make too many waves.

MIN: I'm American! That's what we do!

SHOKO: I'm Japanese! We know when to be quiet.

MIN: I speak my mind! And I don't like people or the government telling me what to do! It kills my spirit!! I gotta be responsible to my spirit.

SHOKO: I don't want you to lose everything. **Mino-san**. Don't make so much noise. Try.

MIN: I'll try. You try too.

SHOKO: Try what?

MIN: Be a little more husband and wifey. *(snuggles)* I'LL GET BY—

SHOKO: No singing!

As they go to bed, non-sexually—

Genovevo starts a small fire in the field.

GENOVEVO: *(to himself)* Burn your own land? What kind of madness?

Then, suddenly, SEARCHLIGHTS scan the sky. ANTI-AIRCRAFT BATTERY GUNS pump into the night. Genovevo looks up. Min runs outside. Shoko, then Arnulfo.

MIN: What the hell?!!

ARNULFO: The Japs have landed!! **Putang ina mo**! I'm too young to die!

MIN: Shuddup!!

Ted enters. SIRENS.

SHOKO *(to GENOVEVO)* What are you burning?!!

GENOVEVO: I-I—

MIN: Go inside!! *(she defies him)* INSIDE!!!

Shoko exits as—

SHERIFF enters, gun drawn.

ARNULFO: Boy am I glad to see you, --

SHERIFF: *(points gun at him)* None of you Japs move a muscle.

ARNULFO: I'm not a Jap, --

SHERIFF: I.D. *(Arnulfo gives him his wallet. Sheriff removes each card dropping them onto the ground. Then the wallet too)* Pick 'em up.

Arnulfo kneels to pick them up.

MIN: What's going on?

SHERIFF: We're under attack! Enemy planes in the sky, submarine sightings off Santa Monica. Bombing Burbank Airport! I'm bringing you all in.

MIN: On what charge?

SHERIFF: Signalling the enemy.

MIN: You kidding?

SHERIFF: Why you burning your crops? Sending smoke signals to your Jap brethren?

MIN: So now we're Indians too?

SHERIFF: Then you'd really be in trouble. What's your name?

MIN: Sitting Pretty.

SHERIFF: Think you're smart, Hatchetface, -- *(as ARNULFO moves away)* Where the hell you going?

ARNULFO: You saw my ID, I'm not—

Sheriff knocks Arnulfo's hat off.

SHERIFF: I say who's a Jap. Now get in line.

Arnulfo picks up his hat, joins line. Genovevo follows suit. Sheriff yanks him away.

SHERIFF: Not you! What are ya, a Nip lover?

MIN: *(to GENOVEVO)* Everything is fine.

SHERIFF: That's what you think. *(to GENOVEVO)* And put out that damn fire!!

Sheriff leads them out. Genovevo starts to put out the fire alone when—

Shoko appears. Using wet sacks of burlap, Shoko smothers the fire. Genovevo joins her.

Together they beat it out, then stamp out the last embers. No words. They breathe hard. They lock eyes. She exits inside. He stays outside.

Scene 3

The GUNS finally subside.

Sunrise. Genovevo stands in the burned field. Still staring, as if Shoko were still there staring back. Silence is broken by—

ESQUINCLE: **Ole**!

Esquincle appears in the distance laughing. Does a fake flamenco dance imitating them putting out the fire.

GENOVEVO: Esquincle! What just happened?

ESQUINCLE: You mean KABOOM?!! The Great Los Angeles Air Raid! No air. No raid! Just a big dream!

GENOVEVO: But the guns, --

ESQUINCLE: Call it a self-inflicted wound!

GENOVEVO: Then we're not at war?

ESQUINCLE: We're in a movie war. Gringos are the cowboys. Which makes the Japaneses the you know who. And me, I got a front row seat at the matinee! I love El Lay!

GENOVEVO: I thought you hit the road.

ESQUINCLE: Too much tequila! Took a snooze under the stars, woke up to War of the Worlds! Chingao! *(beat)* I'm leaving now. Come with me?

GENOVEVO: I can't. *(Genovevo surveys the fields)*

ESQUINCLE: *(whistles)* Buena suerte. You're gonna need it! *(winks)* And leave the dancing to Fred Astaire. Missus Yamada ain't no Ginger Rogers.

Esquincle exits laughing and doing the Mexican hat dance. Genovevo strokes a strawberry plant.

GENOVEVO: **Ay fresa**. If you were mine you'd always come first. You're the beginning and the end and everything in the middle. Whatever I do, I do for you.

Instead of picking the fruit, he kisses a leaf like kissing a woman's hand. As he begins to work, --

They return. Arnulfo tries to fix his hat. Ted massages wrists from handcuff burns. Min has blood around his ear.

ARNULFO: Shouldn't have messed with my hat. This a borsalino, that's what they told me!

Shoko enters.

TED: *(meaning "Look")* Min,....

MIN: *(to SHOKO)* False alarm. The whole thing was a big misunderstanding.

SHOKO: Except the crop burning. *(he looks away)* You heard the Sheriff. We're Japs!

ARNULFO: What about me?

MIN: You're a Flip.

ARNULFO: I'm glad somebody noticed! When I finally convinced them I was Filipino, they called me Manual—as in Manual Labor! In the Philippines I had servants! My servants had servants!

MIN: I pay taxes. I voted for Roosevelt. I scored the winning touchdown for my high school in the City Championship! I am not the enemy! And if they keep treating me like I am, I'm gonna start getting angry!

TED: *(meaning "let's get to work")* Min,....

GENOVEVO: Yeah, Boss. Maybe we should get to work. We already lost the morning—

MIN: That's what they want us to do. Like good little boys and girls. Well we're gonna show them. Shoko. Go to the movies.

SHOKO: I don't want to—

MIN: You're going to the movies. And we're gonna take the rest of the day off. Let's go to town! Beer and cigars!

ARNULFO: Beer sounds mighty fine.

TED: *(meaning "hold on")* Min,....

SHOKO: **Mino-San, --!**

MIN: They're not gonna get our goat!!

Lights change to—

Scene 4

DOWNTOWN LOS ANGELES, 1942. The City. The RED CAR sails by. Noise and jostle. Min, Shoko, Ted, Arnulfo and Genovevo pile out.

Traditional country Mexican CONJUNTO MUSICA plays live—guitar, accordion, bass. Beside it a BAR/CANTINA.

MIN: *(gives SHOKO cash)* Tell Gene Autry I said hi.

SHOKO: **Mottainai**.

MIN: English only, Shoke. Don't want folk thinking your some kinda Mata Hari!

Shoko, silent and frustrated, head down walks away.

GENOVEVO: Boss, I kinda want to see a movie too.

MIN: Gene Autry?

GENOVEVO: The Mexican equivalent. *(MIN winks yes)* **Arigato**, Boss.

MIN : **De nada, amigo**! *(Genovevo exits)* Mexes. Salt of the earth! *(RE: MUSICA)* Listen to that. Happy sad. Laughing and crying. Makes you wanna drink or something.

TED: Or something.

ARNULFO: Let's go get **weng-weng**!

As they go together to the BAR, --

PICHUKA appears. Zoot suit, drape shape, stuffed cuff. Irritated by the MUSICA, sticks fingers in his ears.

PICHUKA: Damn I hate country music! *(as they go by)* **Hierba, Yesca, Amapola**—

Ted stops. The others exit.

TED: *(to PICHUKA)* How much?

Ted extends money in his hand.

PICHUKA: Be cool, fool!

Pichuka makes the connection, supercool sleight of hand. Ted seems to have undergone a personality transfusion.

TED: Ever since Pearl Harbor it's been like pulling teeth just finding joy. Enough to make me go off junk. Well almost.

PICHUKA: You a Farmer John?

TED: That obvious?

PICHUKA: Shitkicker.

TED: You a picker?

PICHUKA: Gimme a break! That's for **pelados**!

TED: Excuse me. You look so sharp if I touch ya I'll cut my hand.

PICHUKA: Why would you wanna touch?

Ted offers his hand to shake. Pause. Pichuka shakes.

TED: Ted. Tetsuro really. *(beat)* Where can I find you?

PICHUKA: Frogtown. Ask for Pichuka. And try not to be so unhep.

TED: Gimme some lessons in cool.

PICHUKA: That would take a lifetime.

Pichuka flips him off, exits. Ted exits the other way. MOVIE MUSIC and HOLLYWOOD DREAMSCAPE as—

GENE AUTRY in a ten gallon hat skyhigh on a movie screen. Sings "AMAPOLA". Shoko looks up at him transfixed. More MOVIE MUSIC as—

JORGE NEGRETE in a big sombrero skyhigh on another movie screen. Sings "JALISCO NO TE RAJES". Genovevo stares up.

As the images flicker out, --

GENOVEVO: **Permiso!**

SHOKO: **Gomennasai!**

GENOVEVO: Good show? *(she nods)* How many times have you seen it?

SHOKO: Six. Three times today. You?

GENOVEVO: *(stars in his eyes)* Just once. Jorge Negrete. Wow. *(clears throat)*
Of course Mister Autry is a fine man.

SHOKO: Hor-hey Ne-gre-te is very handsome.

GENOVEVO: *(beams)* I see Negrete, so tall like a mountain, and I thank God for his life, his voice, his...Mexico. *(beat)* Of course, Gene is a great singer.

SHOKO: Gene has a nice voice.

GENOVEVO: Like Min.

SHOKO: But Min doesn't sing nice songs.

RED CAR comes. Pichuka appears, muy pachucote. Stares at Genovevo. Immediate dislike. Generation Gap 1940s style.

PICHUKA: Take a picture, it'll last longer.

GENOVEVO: **Pachuco**.

PICHUKA: *(grumbles)* **Pelado**!

GENOVEVO: *(to SHOKO)* Hoodlums. Funny clothes. Drugs and gangs. Give **Mejicanos** a bad name—

PICHUKA: You're the Mexican.

GENOVEVO: **Desgraciado!**

PICHUKA: Don't be talking Spanish, see? I don't know none of that jive.

GENOVEVO: *(to SHOKO)* Don't even speak his own language—

PICHUKA: You got something to say, say it to me. Not to the Nippie Chippie.

Genovevo reacts. Shoko holds him back. Pichuka steps to.

PICHUKA: What kinda man are you? You got **bolas**? Got **huevos**? **Me vas a kickear** my ass?!!

SHOKO *(to GENOVEVO)* Don't make waves.

Genovevo backs down.

PICHUKA: That's what burns my **tortas**! You damn hick **campesinos**! Where's your self-pride? **Vete a la madre, padre!**

GENOVEVO: And your drugs? If you were my son you would take off that clown suit, --

PICHUKA: I'm not your son! You're a nobody. A **pelado**! Working the fields 'cause you don't know nothing else! Never own anything! Never be anything --!

SHOKO: *(to PICHUKA)* **BAKA**!!! *(grabs GENOVEVO's arm)* We go home!!

Shoko leads Genovevo away. No nonsense.

PICHUKA: Tough cookie. No wonder the Japs are winning the war.

As the Red Car passes by, --

Scene 5

MIN and ARNULFO at the bar. CONJUNTO MUSICA plays.

MIN: Isn't this great? Gosh I love the City. I belong here.

ARNULFO: How would you make money?

MIN: I'd think of something. Ted and me, we're athletes, singers, actors—all that talent and we're stuck farming!

ARNULFO: Farming takes talent.

MIN: You know what I mean.

ARNULFO: *(ribs him)* Not many chickababes in the fields!

MIN: You said it! *(looks around, stands)* Where's Ted?

A piece of paper falls out of Min's pocket.

ARNULFO: Hey Boss, --

As Arnulfo picks up the paper and reads, --

FBI MAN reappears. Gives voice to the paper.

FBI MAN: WESTERN DEFENSE COMMAND. All Japanese, both alien and non-alien will be evacuated by 12 o'clock noon May 9th.

ARNULFO: That's today! *(reading)* "A responsible member of each family must report to Civil Control Station to receive relocation orders." *(to MIN)* Did you?

MIN: None of your business.

ARNULFO: Boss, the farm is my business.

MIN: No one's gonna take my farm!

ARNULFO: You can say no till the cows come home, you still gotta go.

MIN: What do you know? You never owned nothing!! Leave the business to me.

ARNULFO: *(formal)* Sorry but I'll take my severance Boss.

MIN: You quitting?

ARNULFO: Already called me Jap once. Getting to be a bad habit. *(Min gives him his pay)* I'd like to own something one day. *(tips hat)* Take care Boss. If you're ever up in Fresno, look me up.

Arnulfo walks off. Min reads the notice.

FBI MAN: Qualified operators are needed to supervise the soon-to-be vacated Japanese farms. Those interested please report at once.

MIN: Japanese farms? What's Japanese about my farm? They ain't Japanese strawberries! Just strawberries!!!

MUSICA stops. Min looks around. To everyone:

MIN: I'm not Japanese!!!

Min storms out.

Scene 6

A shanty. Pichuka in underwear clips toenails. Zoot suit on a nail. Radio blares Cab Calloway's "JUMPIN' JIVE."

PICHUKA: *(sings along)* THE JIP-JAM-JUMP IS A JUMPIN' JIVE//MAKES YOU

DIG YOUR JIVE ON THE MELLOW SIDE //THE JIP-JAM-JUMP IS A SOLID JIVE//
MAKES YOU NINE FOOT TALL WHEN YOU'RE FOUR FOOT FIVE, --

Without clothes it is eminently clear that he is a she.

The shanty door opens. Ted appears.

TED: Nice voice, hepcat.

Pichuka, in a fright, shoves the door closed.

PICHUKA: Aintcha never heard of knocking?!!

TED: *(off)* I got cash!

In a mad rush Pichuka hides her hair, throws on a jacket, buttons the top button, forgets to button the rest.

TED: Hey I'm dying here!

PICHUKA: Hold yer horses, **tecato**!!

Pichuka lets Ted in.

TED: Gee thanks.

PICHUKA: *(macho as she can)* That was fast.

TED: I'm celebrating.

PICHUKA: What you got to celebrate?

TED: My freedom. Gimme something I can enjoy right here, right now.

PICHUKA: Where's the **lana**?

TED: *(immitating PICHUKA)* Be cool, fool! *(mock punches her)*

PICHUKA: No touchee my **tacuche! Gabardino, Chino!**

TED: I'm not Chinese.

PICHUKA: Whatever, **Chapo!**

TED: Enough with the pleasantries.

Ted gives cash, gets packet. Uses right there. Snorts.

TED: Oh man you just don't know,....

PICHUKA: **Chale,** I don't even wanna know.

As the drug takes effect, Ted starts to come to life.

TED: Got any girls around here?

PICHUKA: **Rucas**? Sheez! You think the world is your playground?

TED: Yeah. I deserve a little love in my life! I'm over 21. I'm a catch! *(sings)* AMAPOLA, MY PRETTY LITTLE POPPY—Aintcha got no girls stashed around here someplace? I got ants in my pants and I'm itching to dance! Hope some little girl gonna gimme a chance!

PICHUKA: Damn that stuff makes people talk.

Ted gets a bloody nose.

TED: Uh-oh!

PICHUKA: Hey, **Carnal,** don't go dying on my floor, okay?!!

Pichuka sticks a rag up Ted's nose. They are close.

TED: Nice aftershave.

PICHUKA: *(pulls away)* What kinda man are you?

TED: Same as you. Make it up as I go along.

PICHUKA: You looking to get dead?

TED: This stuff don't guarantee long life.

PICHUKA: What you do it for?

TED: Guess I'm just looking for a good place to never wake up.

PICHUKA: Well this ain't it!!

TED: I want out. Of my face, my skin. My name. My dumbass culture. If I could just go to sleep for fifty years. Then when I woke up I could do something else with my life than apologize for being Japanese. *(bows Japanese style)* Goodbye Kid.

PICHUKA: *(curious despite herself)* You going on a trip?

TED: Real special holiday. They take your life away.

PICHUKA: What about the **caballo**? You got it bad. What if you get the shakes?

TED: Play the **maracas** with my teeth I guess. Unless you wanna come along.

PICHUKA: **Chale!**

TED: Thanks for the candy, **Pachuco**.

PICHUKA: Pi-chuka!

TED: Gee that's a pretty name.

Ted exits.

PICHUKA: Whew! *(notices her unbuttoned shirt)* **Ay cabrona**!

Buttons furiously.

Scene 7

The FIELD at sunset. Min squats, hands in dirt. Ted enters. Min gives him a piece of paper. Ted doesn't need to read it.

TED: *(stone cold sober)* What now?

MIN: Report to Santa Anita Racetrack. But we ain't going to see no horses.

TED: We could make a run for it. Pack the flatbed, head out to the desert.
MIN: What about the farm? You want strangers taking over dad's farm?

TED: Why not? You work morn till night and sometimes that ain't enough. Plus you got the champion Ice Queen from Japan giving you the evil eye every time you live a little. This could be the best thing to ever happen to us. We deserve a little freedom in our lives.

MIN: Freedom? They're gonna lock us up!

TED: I mean what you really want. Ask yourself what you really want.

MIN: *(struggles)* I want,....

Shoko and Genovevo enter.

SHOKO: **Mino-San**!!

Min gives her the notice. As she reacts, --

TED: *(to GENOVEVO)* C'mon. Let's leave these kids alone.

Ted and Genovevo start packing.

MIN: How was the movie? *(they stare at each other)* Look, I made a buncha mistakes. And the biggest one was marrying you. *(matter-of-fact)* You're a good wife. You'd do your duty if it killed ya. But you oughta get more outa life than duty.

SHOKO: What have I done wrong?

MIN: Besides settling for me? Ask yourself. *(beat)* Me and Ted gotta go to camp. But I don't want you with us.

SHOKO: But Mino-san, --

MIN: This is what I want! *(for the first time in a long time, he smiles)* It is.

SHOKO: What am I supposed to do?!!

MIN: Here's all the money I got,....

Gives her his wallet. She refuses. He shoves it at her.

MIN: You're gonna need it.

SHOKO: Do you hate me this much?

MIN: You hate me.

SHOKO: I don't!

MIN: You should. I brought you here. And now I can't even offer you a home.

SHOKO: You're my home.

MIN: Not anymore. Maybe not for a long time. So be free.

SHOKO: I don't want to be free!

MIN: I want to be free.

They stare at each other. Shoko bows, very formal. He nods.

MIN: Good. *(calls)* Genovevo!!!

Genovevo enters. Min takes him aside.

MIN: Gimme a dollar.

GENOVEVO: What?

MIN: Gimme a dollar.

Genovevo gives him a crumpled dollar bill.

MIN: Great.

Min gives Genovevo an envelope.

MIN: Here.

GENOVEVO: What?

MIN: Deed to the farm. *(GENOVEVO tries to give it back)* No backs! They're gonna take it from me. But so long as they don't start a camp for Mexes, I'll have a friend in the berry business.

GENOVEVO: But this land is worth—

MIN: Way more than you got. But I'll take your dollar.

SIRENS.

GENOVEVO: You sure about this?

MIN: I don't got time to be sure! *(calls)* SHOKO!!

Min pulls her close, grabs her shawl, wraps her in it, taking pains to cover her face.

MIN: We gotta do this fast.

Shoko stares at him. He looks everywhere but her eyes.

GENOVEVO: Boss, --

MIN: Tell 'em she's your sister.

GENOVEVO: No Boss --!

MIN: She can't be seen! She can't exist! Do this for me.

A SCUFFLE offstage.

TED: *(OFF)* OW! Hey I give up!!!

SHERIFF: *(OFF)* SHUDDUP!

MIN: *(to SHOKO and GENOVEVO)* Do this for me!!!

Genovevo puts an arm around Shoko as—

Sheriff enters, gun drawn on Ted. Behind him THE FBI MAN.

FBI MAN: Minoru Yamada? You are hereby remanded into federal custody.

MIN: Says who?

FBI MAN: Western Defense Command.

MIN: What about my things?

FBI MAN: War Relocation Authority will complete your evacuation. *(sees GENOVEVO and SHOKO)* Who are you?

MIN: **Pelados**. Mexes make good pickers. Nice and cheap, get me?

FBI MAN: *(to GENOVEVO)* Don't leave town. *(to SHOKO)* You neither. *(no response)* Ma'am?

FBI MAN lifts the shawl from her face.

SHOKO: *(beyond weeping)* I just work here.

Silence. Even FBI Man surprised by her force of emotion. Ted looks from Min to Shoko.

TED: *(with sudden energy)* Let's get this show on the road!! *(to MIN)* I'm with ya, Brother.

Min and Ted exit with Sheriff.

TED: *(sings)* I'LL GET BY—

BOTH: AS LONG AS I HAVE YOU!!!

FBI Man lingers, exits. Genovevo and Shoko alone.

GENOVEVO: Missus Yamada. *(no response)* Shoko. I think they're gone.

SHOKO: Take me somewhere. I can't stay here.

As he helps her to her feet and they go, --

Scene 8

Night in the City.

Genovevo walks with Shoko, face hidden beneath the shawl. CONJUNTO MUSICA, lowdown variety, coming from the bar.

GENOVEVO: Beneath the shawl you look like a Mexican. Even to me. You can get lost easier in the City. We need to get you a place to stay. Somewhere they won't look. *(sees a FIGURE in shadow)* **Joven**!

Pichuka steps out of shadow. Puro macho. Very cheeky.

PICHUKA: You got lucky, **pelado**!

Genovevo tries to hide his distaste.

GENOVEVO: You know of any rooms to let?

PICHUKA: By the week the day or the hour?

Genovevo grabs Pichuka by the lapels.

GENOVEVO: We need someplace clean and out of the way and we need it now. Get it?

PICHUKA: Got it. Where's the dough? *(GENOVEVO shows cash)* **Pues, mi casa es su casa!**

As Pichuka leads them away, --

Arnulfo, leaving the bar, sees them. MUSICA recedes as—

Pichuka the real estate agent shows off the shanty.

PICHUKA: Real nice place. No roaches. Least not the kind with legs!

Shoko lies down exhausted on the cot in a fetal position.

GENOVEVO: *(hands over cash)* This is temporary.

PICHUKA: *(winks)* Stay as long as it takes.

GENOVEVO: *(more cash)* And this is to keep it quiet.

PICHUKA: Look, I swallowed my **lengua**!

They look each other over, warily but not unfriendly.

GENOVEVO: Gracias.

PICHUKA: *(drops the act)* Truth be told, I din't always used to be so cool. I din't always wear a reet pleet and a stuffed cuff. When my folks got deported, I was a **pelado** too. Poor, brown, no sense of humor.

GENOVEVO: Truth be told, I didn't always work on a farm. I hung around Frogtown with the **veteranos** who fought for Pancho Villa. We talked the **calico calorama**, like the jive you talk now but cooler, and if you wanted to get it on we'd get it on. So I'm not a total square.

PICHUKA: Why'd you give it up?

GENOVEVO: **La vida loca**? I grew up.

PICHUKA: You got old!

GENOVEVO: Maybe you're right. *(looks at SHOKO)* Life just gets crazier.

PICHUKA: **La vida loca.** *(looking SHOKO over)* Good luck, Romeo. **Cogelo suave**, but if that don't work, just **cogelo**.

Pichuka exits. Silence.

GENOVEVO: Sleep if you can. *(no response)* Things will get better.

SHOKO: Why should they?

GENOVEVO: **Si dios quiere.** If God wills.

SHOKO: Our Gods are not the same.

GENOVEVO: I think they are.

SHOKO: Will they give me back my life?

GENOVEVO: You can ask.

SHOKO: I don't know what to ask for.

GENOVEVO: Ask for what you really need.

Genovevo rises.

SHOKO: **Ma~nana. Si di-os qui-e-re.**

GENOVEVO: **Arigato, Missus Yamada.**

Genovevo exits.

Scene 9

SANTA ANITA RACETRACK ASSEMBLY CENTER, Night.

The Yamadas stand behind barbed wire. Ted's nose is running and his forehead glistens with sweat. Min stays close.

MIN: *(almost like a prayer, talk/sings)* POVERTY MAY COME TO ME, IT'S TRUE BUT WHAT CARE I? SAY, I'LL GET BY, AS LONG AS I—

TED: **Shikata ga nai.**

MIN: Don't talk that stuff.

TED: It can't be helped. Can it?

MIN: BUT WHAT CARE I? SAY I'LL GET BY

Ted spasms feverishly. As MIN holds him, --

THE FIELD, Night. Genovevo kneeds the soil in his hands.

GENOVEVO: Patron. This is how it feels. *(to the soil)* You don't know the difference, do you? My hands feel the same to you. I'm still the same—or am I? *(lies back)* My dreams come true. What am I supposed to dream of now?

As he looks up at the stars, --

THE SHANTY, Night. Shoko bows and prays in severe silence.

SHOKO: Here me, Gods.

Shoko returns to bed. Lies back. Sleeps.LIGHTS CHANGE INTO DREAMSCAPE.
GLOWING LIGHT, Taiko drums and fog all around. Shoko rises. Walks through walls.
Voice loud and clear.

SHOKO: (*no accent*) I want the double feature!!

ONSCREEN AUTRY out of focus. Autry's "AMAPOLA" plays.

SHOKO: Come down off the screen!!!

GENE and his sidekick FROG break through the fog. Played by Min and Ted in cowboy
hats, boots and Western drawl. HORSE WHINNIES. Gene calms his hobby horse.

GENE/MIN: Whoa, Champion.

FROG/TED*: (tres Gabby Hayes)* Yippie!

SHOKO: *(very ingenue)* Gene!!

GENE/MIN: Hullo Miss.

FROG/TED: *(sees SHOKO)* Oh you kid!! A Geisha gal! Back in the saddle again!

SHOKO: Gene, what do I do?!!

GENE/MIN: Don't you worry your pretty little head. Everything's gonna be all right.

She swoons in his arms.

FROG/TED: *(whistles)* Ain't young but she's built for fun!!

SHOKO: Who am I?!! How should I feel? What should I say? Where should I go?!!

GENE/MIN: Just follow the Cowboy Code. Help folks in distress. Respect the law.
Always tell the truth. Works for me.

SHOKO: No one listens! No one sees me.

FROG/TED: *(lecherous)* I see ya.

GENE/MIN: Just keep watching my films, darling. Keep looking up at me. And I'll keep
looking down at you.

HORSE WHINNIES as Gene prepares to exit into the sunset. MUSIC SWELLS as in the
end of a movie.

SHOKO: But I'm here for the double feature!

FROG/TED: Sorry Kid. We're all outa film.

SHOKO: I need more gods! (*Shoko frantically searches the stage*) **Si dios quiere**!!!

ONSCREEN IMAGES FLICKER. JORGE NEGRETE out of focus. Negrete's "JALISCO NO TE RAJES" plays. JORGE NEGRETE and his youthful sidekick PEDRO INFANTE break through the fog. Played by Genovevo and Esquincle in sombreros, charro suits and theeeck Mexican accents. HORSE WHINNIES. Jorge calms his hobby horse.

JORGE/GENOVEVO: **Calmate, chulita.**

PEDRO/ESQUINCLE: **Ayyyyyyy-yi-yiiiii!!!!** (*sees SHOKO*) **Toda madre! Una buenota! Que mamadas!!** (*off AUDIENCE react*) Untranslatable.

JORGE/GENOVEVO: Not to worry. We speak English.

PEDRO/ESQUINCLE: The language of love, **mi flor!**

JORGE/GENOVEVO: Whenever there is injustice—

PEDRO/ESQUINCLE: And a pretty girl, --

JORGE/GENOVEVO: We come to make things right. And maybe sing a couple songs.

PEDRO/ESQUINCLE: And drink a little tequila, --

JORGE/GENOVEVO: We **charros** have more fun. But we're cowboys too. Try us, you'll like us.

GENE/MIN: (*a little stiff*) Hi George.

JORGE/GENOVEVO: (*muy gentilhombre*) Eugenio. You look well.

GENE/MIN: Can't complain.

Frog and Pedro sniff each other like two dogs.

FROG/TED: **Unko!**

PEDRO/ESQUINCLE: **Fuchi!**

GENE/MIN: (*growing perturbed*) Aren't you a little far from your side of the Rio Grande?

JORGE/GENOVEVO: Oh no. We have many aficionados here. *(winks)* Growing every day.

GENE/MIN: Ahem. This particular damsel in distress is one of my fans.

JORGE/GENOVEVO: I'm not so sure.

GENE/MIN: I speak from experience, **amigo**.

SHOKO: *(pointedly to GENE/MIN)* Don't take me for granted. *(to JORGE/GENOVEVO)* What do I do? Will you show me?

PEDRO/ESQUINCLE: I'll show you mine if you show me yours. *(another grito)* **Ella es ruca de pura calentura!! Vamos a desvencigar la cama!!!***(to AUDIENCE)* You don't wanna know.

SHOKO: *(a little ticked off)* I mean will you show me how to make sense of my life!

JORGE/GENOVEVO: *(kneels muy romantico)* A **sus ordenes**!!!

GENE/MIN*: (quite ticked off)* Hey! We're just movie stars here. Sure we try to be role models for the kiddies, but aren't ya kinda putting a lotta weight on an image on a screen?

SHOKO: What other image do we have of God?

All shrug, accept godhead status.

GENE/MIN: Guess you got a point there.

SHOKO: Teach me to be loud and cold and cruel and arrogant and ignorant and selfish and foolish and unstoppable! Teach me to be American!!

JORGE/GENOVEVO: *(unsure)* Hmmmn. To be American,...?

GENE/MIN: You just are. *(RE: the MEXICANS)* Unless you aren't.

JORGE/GENOVEVO: We're Americans! MEXICAN-Americans! We can rope a steer and sing a song as good as any two-bit Roy Rogers, --!!

GENE/MIN: Watch it, Roy's a friend of mine!

PEDRO/ESQUINCLE: We're handsome and gentle to women, we don't drink too much except sometimes, and even if we're kinda stupid machos, it's attractive!!

GENE/MIN: I got no trouble with Mexican people. Don't make me out as the bad guy here!

FROG/TED: He wears a white hat don't forget.

GENE/MIN: I'm just saying Miss, being American isn't something you teach. It's something you're born with. Like a beauty mark. Like loving hotcakes and bacon and not knowing why. Like home.

SHOKO: I have no home.

GENE/MIN: But, --

SHOKO: My home is gone forever.

GENE/MIN: Then I can't help you anymore.

Gene takes off his ten-gallon—now he is firmly Min.

SHOKO: I'm confused.

MIN: This is a shared dream.

SHOKO: I don't want you here! Get out of my dream, Mino-san!!

MIN: I can't help it, it's my dream too.

SHOKO: I don't want to SEE you --!!!

JORGE/GENOVEVO: See me. I will serenade you under the stars, cry in my tequila for the beauty of your eyes, booze and fight and eat **menudo** for your madonna-like virginity!

FROG/TED: Are we talking about the same chippie?

PEDRO/ESQUINCLE: I will teach you the ways of love, --

SHOKO: Is that what I really want?

JORGE/GENOVEVO: It would be fun.

SHOKO: I haven't had fun in a long long time.

Jorge about to kiss her when, --

She closes her eyes. SCREEN flickers. The celluloid jams in the projector and starts to melt and burn.

MIN: Come on Shoke, it's just a dream!

SHOKO: *(Japanese accent returning)* Nothing belongs to me! Not even my dreams!!!

MOVIE MUSIC crashes to a halt. Frog takes off his hat. Now he's Ted. Pedro removes his sombrero. Now Esquincle.

TED: Ah hell. Time for summer camp.

ESQUINCLE: Time to hit the road. **Ya es hora. Puro pedo**!! This brings me down!!

Ted and Esquincle exit. Min, Shoko, and Jorge remain. They stare at each other.

MIN: *(to JORGE)* Dream's over **amigo**. Take your hat off.

JORGE/GENOVEVO: I don't want to.

SHOKO: Why not?

JORGE/GENOVEVO: I don't want the dream to end.

SHOKO: You can dream.

Then CONJUNTO MUSICA—of the slow romantic variety—PLAYED LIVE. Jorge takes his hat off. Now Genovevo.

GENOVEVO: So can you.

They dance slow, and close. Min watches them.

MIN: Where did my dream go?

Min exits into fog. Shoko and Genovevo dance.

END ACT ONE

ACT TWO

SCENE 1

DREAM LIGHT AND CONJUNTO MUSICA.

Genovevo and Shoko dance. He touches her. She touches him. Fog around them recedes. They let go, come apart.DREAM LIGHT AND MUSICA give way to—

SUNRISE. Genovevo pops up from sleeping in the field.

GENOVEVO: **Hijole**!

Blushing, he immediately starts to work. Shoko awakens in the shanty.

SHOKO; **Mino-san!**

Shoko takes a moment to realize where she is. She surprises herself by laughing.

SHOKO: No more **Mino-san**.

She rises. Finds the cracked mirrror. Examines herself.

SHOKO: No more Shoko. *(studies her face)* Are you still there? I don't think so.

Min stands alone at the barbed wire. Frozen. Ted appears, considerably more together than the night before.

TED: Hey Min. *(no response)* Wake up Sleeping Beauty! *(still no response)* I'LL GET BY—

Min finally awakens. Something deeply changed inside him.

MIN: Where did my dream go?

TED: Let's get you inside, --

MIN: It's gone, Ted. I sold it. Now I got nothing. I don't even got a dream!

TED: You got me.

Ted helps him off.

Genovevo weeds with the short hoe.

GENOVEVO: (*wipes sweat from brow*) **Hijo de la chingada**! Some boss you are. Okay, okay. You need a rhythm.

Sings "DAICHI". It doesn't help. Instead he begins to hum then sing "JALISCO NO TE RAJES" and works up a sweat.

GENOVEVO: **JALISCO, JALISCO//JALISCO TU TIENES MI NOVIA// QUE ES GUADALAJARA// MUCHACHA BONITA// LA PERLA MAS RARA //DE TODO JALISCO ES MI GUADALAJARA....**

Esquincle appears. Watches him strain, butt in the air.

ESQUINCLE: *(makes kissing sounds)* **Mamacita**! Move that **colita**!

GENOVEVO: Esquincle! Boy am I glad to see you. Shut your trap and give me a hand.

ESQUINCLE: I wish I could.

GENOVEVO: Come on you lazy bastard, -- *(realizes)* **Ay cabron**! Another dream?

ESQUINCLE: You're living yours. Never thought pigs would fly. But I figured they'd fly sooner than you becoming **patron**!

GENOVEVO: Do I look like a **patron** to you?

ESQUINCLE: You look pretty stinky.

GENOVEVO: I got no crew! Japanese are in camp. Filipinos got scared away. Oakies and Arkies all got drafted or joined up. And not just them. Blacks are peeling potatoes on KP. Mexican Americans are getting shot at on the frontlines. I'm **patron** all right. I'm **patron** alone!

Esquincle shows him a Spanish language newspaper.

ESQUINCLE: **Bracero** Program!

GENOVEVO: **Braceros**?

ESQUINCLE: Alien labor gonna bail you out. **Mejicanos** coming North.

GENOVEVO: What do you mean, **bracero**?

ESQUINCLE: **Braceros! Pelados!** U.S. Government give 'em a passbook, temporary visa. 30 cents an hour, they work all day six days a week! Seven, if you're a **cabeza de culo**—I mean a real **patron**.

GENOVEVO: Thirty cents an hour? Maybe I can get 'em for twenty-five.

ESQUINCLE: **Cabezon de culo**,....

GENOVEVO: But I need help now. Harvest coming. There's nothing worse than seeing fruit die on the vine. **Ayudame, compa**. *(gestures for help)*

ESQUINCLE: I'm not much good anymore,....

Esquincle shows Genovevo his hand. A finger gone.

GENOVEVO: Ay!

ESQUINCLE: Up near Sacra. Rushing for no reason. Oh well. I'll never play piano like Paganinny. *(winks)* Let that be a lesson to you, '**mano**. Don't stick yer fingers where they don't belong!

Esquincle mimes slow dancing with Shoko.

GENOVEVO: Hey! Watch it, **compadre** --!

ESQUINCLE: Hey I'm not the one getting touchy feely with Missus Yamada! Let yer fingers do the sleepwalking? *(GENOVEVO embarrassed)* Don't worry! You were dreaming, that's all. And a man can dream.

GENOVEVO: How far can my dreams go?

ESQUINCLE: **Quien sabe**? From **pelado** to **patron**, and all it took was a little internment. Not quite the way you dreamed it would be, but so what! Dream your ass off! **Si se puede!**

GENOVEVO: **Si se puede.**

Esquincle grabs Genovevo and gives him a kiss.

ESQUINCLE: **Beso!**

Pinches his rear. Genovevo pushes him, or the air, off.

GENOVEVO: Yuck! If you were really here, I'd give you a good **chanclazo**!

ESQUINCLE: I love you too!

Esquincle starts to limp away.

GENOVEVO: Come back, Esquincle. Work with your **compadre**. I could use a good hand.

ESQUINCLE: *(shows the missing finger)* **Compadres** with a **patron**? You've gone to the other side, **cuate. Te cuidas**.

Esquincle is gone. Genovevo stands alone in the sun.

GENOVEVO: **Braceros**, eh? But I need help NOW. *(to the plants)* This, **fresitas**, is the moment of truth. *(to himself)* **Caray**! What the hell am I gonna do?!!

Arnulfo appears in city clothes. Genovevo does not immediately recognize him.

ARNULFO: Psst. Hey! It's me! Manual Labor.

GENOVEVO: Arnulfo! Thought you went to Fresno.

ARNULFO: Why go to Fresno if you don't have to?

GENOVEVO: Cops still think you're Japanese?

ARNULFO: That's what's great about being Filipino. When the Oriental thing gets old, well you can always go Spanish. And if that don't work, --

Arnulfo shows a button on his lapel—"I AM FILIPINO."

GENOVEVO: You're here just in time.

ARNULFO: We need to renegotiate. I scratch your back, you scratch mine.

GENOVEVO: Why should I scratch your back?

ARNULFO: I saw you with Missus Yamada,.... *(GENOVEVO freezes)* Let's have a drink. You're buying.

Beat. Genovevo removes a bottle of tequila.

SCENE 2

Shoko stands at the mirror.

SHOKO: I'm nobody. Who are you? *(beat)* No name. No face. You're smoke.

In the mirror she sees, or thinks she sees, Min.

MIN: But you're free.

SHOKO: Free?

MIN: I'm not free.

SHOKO: I went out today. Hid beneath the shawl you shackled me to. Didn't have to say a single word. No one cared. Beneath this I'm just another Mexican. This is the freedom you gave me.

MIN: Okay. Nobody's free. *(trying to be cheerful)* Seen any movies lately?

SHOKO: No more movies.

MIN: Shoke, I'm—I'm sorry—

Without knocking, Pichuka enters. Half in drag, half out.

PICHUKA: **Que desmadre!**

Shoko grabs the shawl to hide. Too late.

SHOKO: Get out!

PICHUKA: This is my **casita**.

They recognize each other unmasked.

PICHUKA: Hey! You're the Nippie Chippie!

SHOKO: You're the Pa-chu-ko!

PICHUKA: Pi-chu-ka!! Guess the gato's outa the bag. Trick or treat!

Shoko tosses the shawl aside.

SHOKO: No sense hiding now. I'm worn out.

PICHUKA: I'M worn out. **Acabado—acabada**—whatever! Maybe it's my time of the moon. No fun when you're wearing a drape shape with a stuff cuff.

Pichuka flops on the cot.

SHOKO: Skirts are easier.

PICHUKA: But they're not reet. Girly girl's no good on the street.

SHOKO: Neither is Japanese.

PICHUKA: You hiding too?

SHOKO: I'm the invisible woman.

PICHUKA: Cool.

SHOKO: If they see my face it's not so cool.

PICHUKA: Oh shit! That's what happened to Ted!

SHOKO: You know Ted?

PICHUKA: Don't worry, it's not like we slept together. He thinks I'm a guy!

Shoko stares at Pichuka like some kind of exotic bird.

SHOKO: Why do you dress like—like --?

PICHUKA: Business.

SHOKO: I hate business.

PICHUKA: You must hate this country. 'Cause that's what it's all about. **Negocios**, baby. I dress cool 'cause my business demands a certain **como-se-llama**. Style and substances. But if I come in second-class, in a dress like some old lady making beans, I'll be solid broke in a hot minute. Off the cob. Square as a jeff. Bad business. But this way I'm **pachucote, suavecito**, The Man.

SHOKO: But you're not.

PICHUKA: I know, but— (*suddenly near tears*) I'm just a little tired, that's all!

Long beat. Finally Shoko softens.

SHOKO: Be who you are.

Shoko lets Pichuka's hair down. Pichuka is revealed as a beautiful young woman.

SHOKO: Are you all alone?

PICHUKA: All the men are gone, joined up or in jail, all the warriors gone to war and

I'm so damn lonely! And I'll be damned if I sit around crying and waiting! Someone gotta take care of business. *(laughs through tears)* But this get-up is getting me down.

SHOKO: These clothes really fool people?

PICHUKA: Fooled Ted.

SHOKO: He is a fool.

PICHUKA: I think he's cute.

SHOKO: *(fingers the zoot suit)* They give you a new face.

PICHUKA: Well it helps I'm not too chesty,....

SHOKO: Maybe they can give me one too.

PICHUKA: You? A Zooter? I don't think so!

SHOKO: A working man's clothes, --

PICHUKA: You got curves in all the wrong places, it ain't never gonna work.

SHOKO: I'll make it work. I need to be free.

PICHUKA: You think it'll make you free?

SHOKO: Anything will be an improvement.

PICHUKA: *(looks her over, shrugs)* Let's wrap that bosom of yours,....

Pichuka starts to tailor a new look on Shoko.

SHOKO: Pach-uko no. But a working man,....

PICHUKA: **Pelado!**

SHOKO: What is pe-la-do?

PICHUKA: He's pure square. **Jefe** says jump, he says how high? Goes to bed early Saturday night so he can pray all day Sunday. Sends all his cash back home to **Me-ji-co** and don't got enough **pesos** in his pocket for a beer. Cries when he hears Negrete sing about Guadala-whatsis, dreams he's some kinda cowboy **de aquellas**! Straight off the cob!

SHOKO: That's the kind of man I wanna be.

PICHUKA: Then a **pelado** you shall be.

Pichuka gives Shoko her worst clothes. Shoko somehow wears them well—with dignity.

PICHUKA: **Esa!** It ain't my style, but for some crazy reason it suits you!

Pichuka gives her a dented hat to hide her hair.

PICHUKA: **Hijo 'mano!** Everything but the moustache. You almost fool me. Of course, you're not as good a man as me! My disguise is foolproof!

SHOKO: I knew.

PICHUKA: Knew what?

SHOKO: The first time. When you made all that noise. No man would do that.

PICHUKA: Yeah? Well you got the last word and it wasn't quiet neither.

SHOKO: Women usually get the last word.

PICHUKA: I was kinda **celoso** when I saw you with that fine Mexican dinner.

SHOKO: Ce-lo-so?

PICHUKA: Jealous, **chavala!**

SHOKO: Of what fine dinner?!!

PICHUKA: Damn you're square! Your squeeze!

SHOKO: My what?!!

PICHUKA: Tall dark and handsome! I'd like to give him a piece of my mind or something,....

SHOKO: Genovevo? He's not my— *(after a beat)* I thought you didn't like him!

PICHUKA: That's how I talk to all the guys. He burns my ass being so macho—but it's kinda sexy. If he weren't such a Farmer John, he'd be a real Hollywood heartthrob. But why I gotta tell you? You know all about it, --!

SHOKO: I don't know anything!

PICHUKA: **Puro pedo.**

SHOKO: Pe-do?

PICHUKA: There's a word for you. I can teach you a buncha good ones.

SHOKO: **Pedo**?!!

PICHUKA: That's right.

SHOKO: **PEDO**.

PICHUKA: **Con huevos!!**

SHOKO: **PEDO!!!!**

PICHUKA: Nuff said. Sure the world gets tough. But that's when we chicks get going. *(beat)* What's your name anyways?

SHOKO: Shoko.

PICHUKA: Choko?

SHOKO: Shoko.

PICHUKA: Weird...but cool.

A knock. Then Genovevo and Arnulfo enter.

GENOVEVO: *(surprised, not recognizing either)* **Permiso**.

PICHUKA: Come on in, it's a party.

GENOVEVO: **Buenos dias**.

ARNULFO: *(to PICHUKA)* **Buenas nachos!**

Shoko takes off hat. Her hair falls onto her shoulders.

GENOVEVO: Shoko!

ARNULFO: *(tips hat)* Missus Yamada. *(to PICHUKA)* Is this a dress up party? Can I play? I look pretty good in hose!

GENOVEVO: Shoko, you have to hide—

SHOKO: No. No more hiding. *(introduces PICHUKA)* She knows everything already.

GENOVEVO: Loose lips sink ships.

PICHUKA: Look, I swallowed my **lengua**!

Genovevo double-takes. Pichuka chuckles.

GENOVEVO*: (clears throat)* It's harvest time.

ARNULFO: **Wow cubao**! We're back in business!

SHOKO: Business? **Pedo**!

GENOVEVO: Missus Yamada!

SHOKO: **Puro pedo**!

GENOVEVO: I need you. *(beat)* I mean, I need every hand.

ARNULFO: There's a phrase with my people—**Tayong Lahat**. It means all of us. That's what it's gonna take.

GENOVEVO : As bad as things may be, Spring means work. Summer, harvest. We gotta a lotta work to do! *(beat)* Please.

SHOKO: I will come. But on condition. *(returns hat on head)* I come as a **pelado**.

GENOVEVO: I don't understand, --

ARNULFO: Great disguise! No one looks at the pickers. Keep that hat on and a scarf over your face and you could be anybody! You'll fool the cops sure!

SHOKO: Not just the cops. If I come, you will treat me as a **pelado**. Your **her-man-o**.

GENOVEVO: **Hermano**?

She nods. As they stare at each other, --

ARNULFO: *(winks to PICHUKA)* Hey **maganda**! Why not come join us too?

PICHUKA: You gotta be kidding.

ARNULFO: Women make good pickers. They don't bruise the fruit.

PICHUKA: Real funny.

GENOVEVO: We need every hand.

PICHUKA: *(sexily)* What do you need it for?

GENOVEVO: *(needling)* You know what they say about **pachucos**.

PICHUKA*: (angering)* What do they say?

GENOVEVO: They say they're afraid to WORK.

PICHUKA: BullCACA!!!

GENOVEVO: **No saben trabajar. Puros vacilones—**

PICHUKA: I know how to work, I can work my titties off!

GENOVEVO: Then show us.

A beat. They all look at each other.

PICHUKA: I make more money on the corner in a day than you make in a month on your stinky farm.

SHOKO: But you can be yourself. *(quotes her)* When the world gets tough, we chicks get going.

PICHUKA: I could use a vacation from the street. **Ya me aguite!** *(beat)* Trial basis.

GENOVEVO: Non-binding.

PICHUKA: Cool.

They all shake hands.

ARNULFO: *(to GENOVEVO)* **Compadre.**

GENOVEVO: *(to ARNULFO)* **Compadre.**

SHOKO: *(to PICHUKA)* **Compadre.**

PICHUKA: *(to SHOKO)* **Comadre!** *(to ARNULFO)* **A toda madre!**

As they laugh, Shoko prays.

GENOVEVO: What did you pray?

SHOKO: **Tencho chikyu fu-u junji**. *(translates)* Long life to heaven and earth and may the winds and the rains bless us. *(translates again)* **Si Dios quiere.**

GENOVEVO: **Si Dios quiere.**

Shoko looks at Genovevo and sees—

Min in the mirror.

MIN: Every harvest I used to wish I was somewhere else. Now I am somewhere else,... I wish I was there. *(beat)* When the wind blows, that'll be me.

Min disappears. The wind blows.

SHOKO; **Kamisama.**

GENOVEVO: Missus Yamada?

SHOKO: *(a breath, then)* Let's go to work.

As Shoko, Pichuka and Arnulfo head towards the FIELDS—

SCENE 3

A QUEUE of BRACEROS. MACIAS among them.

FBI Man appears. Voice of the official agreement:

FBI MAN: AGREEMENT for the temporary migration of Mexican Agricultural Workers to the United States—

FLASH! as MACIAS's photo is taken.

FBI MAN: Contracts will be made between the employer and the worker under the supervision of the Mexican Government.

Macias strips. INS MAN sprays him with white powder.

INS MAN: Kills fleas.

MACIAS: *(coughs)* You have bad fleas up here?

INS MAN: Who taught you to speak American?

MACIAS: Gene Autry!

FBI MAN: Wages for hourly work will not be less than 30 cents per hour.

Macias puts clothes on. INS MAN gives him a paper bag.

INS MAN: Baloney sandwich.

MACIAS: **Que gloria**! *(takes a big bite)* What kind of meat is baloney?

INS MAN: You don't wanna know.

FBI MAN: At the expiration of the contract, the authorities of the United States shall consider the continued stay of the worker ILLEGAL.

FBI Man recedes. Genovevo enters.

GENOVEVO: I filled out the paperwork.

INS MAN: Sign here. *(as he does)* You a Messican?

Before Genovevo can answer, --

MACIAS: **Patron**? *(shakes hands)* Macias!

GENOVEVO: **Bienvenidos** a California!

MACIAS: Speak English! It's okay.

GENOVEVO: Where are you from, Macias?

MACIAS: Jalisco.

GENOVEVO: Jalisco?!! *(a GRITO)* **Pues** come on!

As Genovevo leads Macias and OTHER BRACEROS away, --

INS MAN: Sure excited about a buncha stinking brazers.

GENOVEVO; Smells sweet to me.

INS MAN: It would, wouldn't it. *(sniffs the air)* You Mexes don't wash, do ya? Guess that's what comes of sleeping in dirt. What else do ya do in the dirt? *(laughs)* I got one for ya. What do ya get when you cross a Mex and a Nigra? Someone who's too lazy to steal! *(laughs)* I got another! A Mex and a Nigra are in a car. Who's driving? The Police!

As he laughs, --

Genovevo begins to CURSE. At first under his breath. Then gaining momentum. Macias, then the other Braceros, join him. It becomes a kind of FUGUE of expletives, musical, rhythmic, starting angry but growing strangely beautiful.

INS MAN: You say something?

GENOVEVO: We said thanks.

MACIAS: Spanish is a flowery language.

As they go, smiling to themselves, --

THE FIELD. Shoko, Arnulfo and Pichuka do stoop labor. Pichuka in overalls. Shoko beneath scarf and big hat.

PICHUKA: Vacation?!! What was I thinking?!! I think I just busted my sacroiliac!!

SHOKO: We barely started.

PICHUKA: When do we get paid? *(ARNULFO laughs at her)* What are you laughing at?

Genovevo leads the Braceros into the field. They stand around, shy, awkward.

PICHUKA: Who the hell are these **pelados**?

Arnulfo pulls out a flask. Offers the Braceros.

ARNULFO: **Kampai!**

MACIAS: Compay?

ARNULFO: Close enough.

They drink.

GENOVEVO: **Companeros**! You have come a long way North from Mexico.

PICHUKA: Gimme a break.

GENOVEVO: The road is hard. I know the journey well, --

PICHUKA: Yeah you swim like hell, --

SHOKO: **Urasai yo!**

PICHUKA: You telling me to shut up?

SHOKO: You're learning Japanese.

MACIAS: Patron! You must be a great man. A **ranchero**, and a **Mejicano**! I will work hard to make you proud of me!

PICHUKA: The ultimate brown-nose.

SHOKO: Sssh!!

GENOVEVO: **Vamos a trabajar**!

They move towards a pile of short handled hoes. Genovevo nods to Arnulfo who passes out long handled hoes instead.

GENOVEVO: Use these instead.

SHOKO: **A-mendokusai**! Don't, --

PICHUKA: *(to SHOKO)* **U**rasai yourself!

SHOKO: We'll bruise the fruit!

GENOVEVO: Better the fruit than you.

SHOKO: Baka!

ARNULFO: My back thanks you. *(to EVERYONE)* Careful with the fruit! **Cuidado! Pag-ingatan!**

SHOKO: *(mutters to GENOVEVO)* Stupid, stupid, stupid.

PICHUKA: *(to SHOKO)* What do you care? Ain't your farm.

They arrange themselves in rows.

ARNULFO: Hey Boss. We need a rhythm.

Shoko begins to sing "DAICHI".

SHOKO: **AIN-YA COLASHO//DOC-COISHO//NUNNO COLASHO//AIN-YA COLLASHO//BOC-COISHO//NUNNO-COLASHO....**

The Braceros stand there.

GENOVEVO: What's wrong?

MACIAS: We don't know that song.

GENOVEVO: What do you know?

The Braceros whisper among themselves.

MACIAS: Bueno, -- *(sings full out)* **AY JALISCO, JALISCO, JALISCO//
TU TIENES MI NOVIA// QUE ES GUADALAJARA!!**

GENOVEVO/MACIAS: **MUCHACHA BONITA// LA PERLA MAS RARA//
DE TODO JALISCO ES MI GUADALAJARA!!**

ARNULFO: Sounds good to me!

The Braceros work. Shoko stands alone, out of rhythm. Suddenly Pichuka joins her.
PICHUKA: *(loud)* Turn up the radio or something!! *(SONG stops)* That's old fogey
musica! Gimme a beat, something we can jitterbug to. Come on, put some pep in it!!
(scat-sings) FROM THE FURROW OF MY BROW I DON'T WANNA HOE AND
PLOW, I JUST WANNA DANCE A LITTLE, COME ON BOY, LET'S SHAKE AND
JIGGLE, I JUST WANNA DO THE JITTERBUG!

Pichuka jitterbugs in the middle of the field.

MACIAS: Too much sun!

PICHUKA: You **Indios** oughta understand! Them **Aztecas** and **Toltecas** and **Olmecas**
did some crazy ass dancing in their time! And they did it buck naked!!

GENOVEVO: Better left in the past. But if you can keep a beat, we'll work to it. (beat)
With clothes.

Macias and the Braceros shake their heads no.

MACIAS: **Por favor**, --

ARNULFO: Boss, we're way outa rhythm,....

Before Genovevo can reply, --

SHOKO: *(sings best she can)* **JALISCO, JALISCO, JALISCO, JALISCO,
JALISCO—** *(stops)* Help me out, it's all I know!

EVERYONE: *(except PICHUKA)* **TU TIENES MI NOVIA QUE ES
GUADALAJARA!!**

PICHUKA: **Pelados.**

As they work, --

Genovevo steps away. Straightens his clothes.

GENOVEVO; *(to ARNULFO)* Take over.

PICHUKA: Where you going?

GENOVEVO: I just, -- *(beat)* It's business. **Tu sabes.**

ARNULFO: Right. **Patron.**

Arnulfo takes over the foreman's place.

PICHUKA: Business! *(to GENOVEVO as he goes)* **A la chingada con** your business!

Genovevo watches them work from the porch.

GENOVEVO: *(feels his back)* Haven't stood this straight for years.

Dream Esquincle joins Genovevo, limping, coughing.

ESQUINCLE: **Hijo de la guayaba**! Is this Mexico? Did I take a wrong turn at Riverside?

GENOVEVO: I'm just getting used to it myself.

ESQUINCLE: *(surveys the fields)* Looks like it used to. When California belonged to us.

GENOVEVO: We weren't even born yet, **baboso.**

ESQUINCLE: This is the beginning of something. I don't know what, but it's the beginning of something! Thank God for these **Braceros**, no?

GENOVEVO: Just like we used to.

ESQUINCLE: I'm still doing it! *(coughs into a handkerchief)*

GENOVEVO: Are you sick?

ESQUINCLE: Just a little T.B. *(off GENOVEVO's react)* What do you expect? Winters get cold, desert nights you freeze your **huevos**!

GENOVEVO; Warm by the fire. Come live with me, --

ESQUINCLE: **Ay que coqueto eres!!**

GENOVEVO: Come work here.

ESQUINCLE: You got enough Mexicans. *(coughs)*

GENOVEVO; Esquincle! Don't die.

ESQUINCLE: Die? We **donnadies** live forever.

GENOVEVO: **Donnadie?**

ESQUINCLE: Nobodies! Losers. But that's just me. You on the other hand are a **casinadie**.

GENOVEVO: Real VIP.

ESQUINCLE: They think you are.

Genovevo stares at Shoko.

GENOVEVO: What does she think?

ESQUINCLE: Ask her.

GENOVEVO: I can't.

ESQUINCLE: Cat got your **lengua?** *(ribs him)* Enjoy yourself, **compadre!** Have fun. I never tasted **sushi**, --

GENOVEVO: **Callete o te rompo la jeta!!**

ESQUINCLE: Tell me you haven't thought about it!

GENOVEVO: I think about it all the time!

ESQUINCLE: I was starting to worry! *(ribs him)* You like your **chicas** in pants, huh?

GENOVEVO: I feel like a kid. I'm even blushing! My whole life I've worked. But tonight, -- *(stares at SHOKO)* Tonight I'll try to put down my tools.

ESQUINCLE: Don't put 'em all down. Live life, **compadre**. Let's see what kind of Latin lover you really are.

Esquincle pushes Genovevo towards Shoko.

GENOVEVO: Missus— *(clears throat)* Shoko.

She keeps working. Anger simmering.

SHOKO: Call me **pelado**.

GENOVEVO: It's not who you are.

SHOKO: Call me **pelado**.

GENOVEVO: I'm trying to take care of you!!

SHOKO: Don't.

GENOVEVO; It's my business!

SHOKO: Go back to your business.

GENOVEVO: You are my business!

SHOKO: I'm not anyone's business!

The OTHERS look up from their work.

GENOVEVO: *(embarrassed, to THEM)* Everyone back to work! *(to SHOKO)* I know what's underneath the shawl!

SHOKO : In your dreams.

She returns to stoop labor. Genovevo returns to watching from afar. Esquincle joins him.

ESQUINCLE; Real Romeo.

Genovevo exits. DREAMLIGHT as—

SCENE 4

They work.

TED appears—very early Frank Sinatra. He walks among them, invisible, godlike.

TED: *(sings)* IT ISN'T FAIR FOR YOU TO TAUNT ME//HOW CAN YOU MAKE ME CARE THIS WAY//IT ISN'T FAIR FOR YOU TO WANT ME//IF IT'S JUST FOR TODAY

Genovevo stares at Shoko. Ted seems to speak for him.

TED: IT ISN'T FAIR FOR YOU TO THRILL ME//WHY DO YOU DO THE THINGS YOU DO?//IT ISN'T FAIR FOR YOU TO THRILL ME//WITH THOSE DREAMS THAT CAN'T COME TRUE

PICHUKA: Look at him. **Patron** growing callouses on his ass from sitting. Just 'cause he owns the place. Asshole!

ARNULFO: But by God he's our asshole. *(winks)* One day you'll be boss. And I shudder to think what kind of pain in the butt you will be to the rest of us.

TED: *(big Hollywood finish)* IT ISN'T FAIR!!!

As he exits, --

Shoko looks up from her work.

SHOKO: **Mino-san**! This is as free as I can be. Working. My head down and my back bent. Sunrise to twilight. And no dreams. No thoughts of you,... or any other man. I don't have to be Japanese. I hardly have to be human. *(beat)* Is this what you wanted, **Mino-san**?

TAIKO DRUMS, with an edge. Min enters, almost unrecognizeable. Bedecked in kimono, sandals and samurai sword. Very Toshiro Mifune.

SHOKO: **Mino-san**!

MIN: *(grunts)*

SHOKO: You look....wonderful.

MIN: *(GRUNTS, then)* I feel like hell. No wonder them oldtime Japanese never smile. Goddamn robe keeps riding up my butt. Gimme a pair of jeans any day. And this? (removes samurai sword) It would be nice to kill some **hakujin**.

Min does a series of kendo moves, very SEVEN SAMURAI.

SHOKO: It will have to live in dreams.

MIN: *(grunts)*

SHOKO: I've never seen you like this.

MIN: *(grunts)*

SHOKO: So...few words! I like it. Strong and silent, gruff and dark.

MIN: Like Genovevo.

SHOKO: What?!!

MIN: A man with dreams.

SHOKO: No!!

MIN: A man.

SHOKO: What are you telling me?!!

Min grabs her by hair, very sexual, very hot.

MIN: *(grunts)*

Taikos bang like crazy. LIGHTS CHANGE BACK. Min exits. Shoko turns to see Genovevo staring at her. He turns away.

SCENE 5

THE FIELD transforms, harvest complete. Shoko boxes the last of the berries. Arnulfo apperas. He sports a new hat.

ARNULFO: **'Tang 'na**! I hate packing crates. But I love them once they're packed!

Genovevo removes a cash wad. Counts out Arnulfo's share.

GENOVEVO: Good work, partner.

ARNULFO: Worked hard. Worked our **titis** off.

Genovevo counts out a couple extra bills.

GENOVEVO: Foreman gets a little extra.

ARNULFO: Fine by me. Everyone moves up a notch. Some guys don't even have to break their back.

GENOVEVO: *(a touch defensive)* I had paperwork, taxes. Someone had to sell the berries, --

ARNULFO: I know the business. But some people kinda missed you out in the fields.

GENOVEVO: Stay for a drink?

ARNULFO: *(shakes head no)* Filipino Brotherhood holding a **fiesta**. **Adobo**, sticky rice—and lots of gambling! Mah jong, fan tan, craps!!

GENOVEVO: Didn't know you were a gambler.

ARNULFO: Didn't have the cash. Thanks to you, I found the real me!

Arnulfo exits. Genovevo stands near Shoko, unable to begin conversation. Just as he is about to speak, --

PICHUKA: When the hell do we get paid?

GENOVEVO: Right now.

Genovevo gives her cash.

PICHUKA: This is it?

GENOVEVO: I never said you'd get rich.

PICHUKA: I don't mean the money. I thought— *(breaks off)* I thought it would be different.

GENOVEVO: This is the way it always is.

PICHUKA: That's what I mean. When we shook hands as compadres I thought—I thought—I was stupid.

GENOVEVO: I treat you like I treat anyone.

PICHUKA: Any other picker. Any other **pelado**. I thought you'd treat me like family....

GENOVEVO: This is business. *(offers more cash)* Wait. Don't go away mad, --

PICHUKA: Nix! Man, I thought you was hep. Now I see you're sadder than a map.

GENOVEVO: You said you worked the fields before.

PICHUKA: I got no problem with the fields! It's the system! Somebody always gotta be the Boss. Always someone gotta be above the rest. I thought you'd be one of us. One of us!

GENOVEVO: I am.

PICHUKA: You were.

GENOVEVO: Is it really any better on the street?

PICHUKA: No. That's what's so sad. **Hay te watcho**. See you when I see you.

Pichuka splits. Macias approaches Genovevo.

MACIAS: *(RE: PICHUKA)* Mexican-Americans. For them the pain is so fresh. Injustice so unjust. We **Mejicanos** have perspective. Our dreams didn't come true either. But our tears are nothing new. We've been crying for five hundred years.

GENOVEVO: Has it been so bad here?

MACIAS: Los Angeles is wonderful! Just like Mexico, only with money! So many beautiful Mexican people everywhere! Washing dishes in every restaurant, taking care of the **chavalillos**, and of course out in the fields **trabajando**!

GENOVEVO: I mean here. The farm. The work.

MACIAS: It's work.

Genovevo gives Macias cash. Macias surprised how little.

GENOVEVO: The rest will be in your account on the Mexican side.

MACIAS: But we don't return to Mexico, we have another job in Northern California!

GENOVEVO: That's the contract.

Macias, about to argue, instead nods and smiles sadly.

MACIAS: Maybe it's better to cry loud. Five hundred years is a long time to wait.

GENOVEVO: I wish I could do more,....

MACIAS: It's the business, **Patron**. *(beat)* See you next harvest.

GENOVEVO: Yes?

MACIAS: Next year I bring my **hermanito**!

Macias exits. Only Genovevo and Shoko.

GENOVEVO: Missus Yamada?

SHOKO: *(returns)* Shoko.

Shoko, hair down, holds kimono outstretched for him. A perplexed Genovevo strips off jacket, then shirt, then jeans. Puts on kimono. Unused to it he gets an arm stuck.

GENOVEVO: Little tight, no?

SHOKO: Sit.

Genovevo attempts to sit cross-legged Asian style.

SHOKO: *(rises)* I'm preparing a bath.

GENOVEVO: Shower's fine.

SHOKO: Japanese-style. Wash first with soap. Then we soak and relax.

GENOVEVO: We?

SHOKO: f you want.

GENOVEVO: **Mi casa su—**

They kiss.

GENOVEVO: Shoko, I—

SHOKO: Come.

As they kiss Hollywood style, --

SCENE 6

MOVIE MUSIC swells. Snippets of RADIO and NEWSREEL take us through the Year 1943. Into 1944. Genovevo and Shoko remain lip-locked.

An older wiser Macias leads the Braceros to work. Arnulfo appears, dressed for gambling, not for work.

ARNULFO: Macias. **Que pasa, 'mano?**

MACIAS: Don't see you using your **manos.**

ARNULFO: No **pisca** for me. These are gambler's hands. Now that you're foreman I got time to live, and bucks in my pocket to spend! War is profitable! Couple good crops, plus you brazers working on the cheap, and suddenly farming ain't so hard!

MACIAS: Maybe not for you.

ARNULFO: Where's da Boss?

MACIAS: His manos are pretty busy right now.

ARNULFO: What's the Boss doing?

MACIAS: You know what. *(mimes smooching)*

ARNULFO: Don't they ever get tired? Took 'em forever to get together. It'll take a crowbar to pull 'em apart.

Finally they pull apart. Share a blush. As she goes in, Genovevo lights a cigar and looks out at the fields.

ARNULFO: *(watching THEM)* How's your love life?

MACIAS: That's a good one. They have a sign at the bar NO DOGS NEGROES MEXICANS. Call us deportees. I go to a taxi dance, spend my money for a cup of bilge beer and a peroxide blonde. After all these months I'm not complaining. Anyway the girls are used to the way I smell. Of the earth. They let me hold them around the waist when the trio plays **conjunto**. The music takes me home.

ARNULFO: Season's almost over. Dontchu Braceros gotta get back to wherever the hell?

MACIAS: If we want our money.

ARNULFO: Got ya by the short and curlies. *(beat)* Supper ready yet? **Carnitas** and **sushi!** **Tempura tacos!** I love the way Shoko cooks these Mexican **fiestas**.

MACIAS: Not just any fiesta. Mexican Independence Day.

ARNULFO: You guys independent? That's a good one.

Esquincle appears, hunchbacked, old before his time. When he speaks, Esquincle sounds different, more tired.

ARNULFO: *(to MACIAS, gesturing)* Mister **Weng-Weng!**

ESQUINCLE: *(to GENOVEVO)* Look like the cat who got the **crema!**

GENOVEVO: Esquincle?

ESQUINCLE: Well it ain't Cantinflas!

GENOVEVO: You a dream?

ESQUINCLE: This flesh is all too real, **compadre**.

They embrace.

GENOVEVO: I don't know what's real anymore.

ESQUINCLE: These **fresas** are real.

GENOVEVO: Where you been?

ESQUINCLE: Utah! Those Mormons work harder than the Japanese! And you can't get a drink to save your life! I almost died of thirst! When I crossed the state line that first tequila tasted good! Got under a **nopal**, tipped my hat over my eyes, and slept like a baby. Like a stone. Like I'd never wake up again.

GENOVEVO: Sleep here. Long as you want.

ESQUINCLE: Nah! I'm just passing through. Just came to say **Vaya con Dios**! You were right. The road is long. And hard!!

GENOVEVO: You got to see the world.

ESQUINCLE: It made me old. *(beat)* Such is life, eh **Patron**? *(pulls out a bottle of tequila)* One for the road?

GENOVEVO: One more can't hurt too bad!

They drink.

ESQUINCLE: **Y tu**. Used to have the worst case of lackanooky I ever seed. Now you got a smile on ya that can mean only one thing. Who's the unlucky woman?

GENOVEVO: You don't know?

ESQUINCLE: You dreaming? How could I? Haven't seen you since, --

GENOVEVO: Right. Stay for supper **compadre**. For old times sake.

ESQUINCLE: I'll stay 'cause I'm hongry! *(stretches lazily)* **Entonces**, -- You don't mind if maybe I do catch a couple ZZZs, -- *(laughs)* When I wake up, I'm gonna dance. I'm gonna dance the **taconazo**, the happy dance. 'Cause this is one war we won. *(winks)* **Patron**!

GENOVEVO: I held onto the farm. Tried to do business without giving anyone the business. That's all.

ESQUINCLE: Farming is luck. You got lucky! First time one of us got lucky since Cortez kissed La Malinche! *(beat)* My luck stayed bad. **Tortilla duras**, not even good enough for beans! You stayed right here, lucky dog. Who knew? **Asi es la vida**.

They embrace. Esquincle exits.

CONJUNTO MUSICA. Genovevo lights a cigar.

Pichuka appears. Back in urban get-up but no longer hiding her sex. Perhaps the best she has ever looked.

PICHUKA: What's up, **Patron**!

GENOVEVO: Pichuka. You look...good.

PICHUKA: You think? Instead of taking things apart, I thought I'd put 'em all together. Embrace confusion, tu sabes? It's a statement. Taffeta just ain't for me, but I'm tired of hiding these *(her breasts)*

GENOVEVO: You still mad at me?

PICHUKA: For being a butthead? Life is too short. I'm a bit of a **patrona** myself these days. My business is picking up like gangbusters.

GENOVEVO: Amapola?

PICHUKA: It's all drugs, one kind or another. That's not really the business we do.

GENOVEVO: We?

PICHUKA: You're a helluva businessman. I learned a lot last summer on the farm. And I put it to use in the city. Treat my clients just like growing a crop.

GENOVEVO: I just sell berries.

PICHUKA: And you bought 'em for a dollar. *(winks)* We buy despair. We sell certainty. That's the American way. Troops are coming home, half of 'em are hopheads. I got a crew of **chavalas** working the streets for me, don't even gotta get my hands dirty. You and me? We come a long way, baby.

Shoko appears.

SHOKO: Supper's almost ready!! **A comer!!**

PICHUKA: **Orale** Choko!

SHOKO: Hey Crazy Girl! Help me in the kitchen.

PICHUKA: I'm hooked on that sticky Japanese rice of yours.

SHOKO: *(with a nod at GENOVEVO)* I make Spanish rice now.

PICHUKA: Hubba hubba.

Pichuka winks at Genovevo, about to exit with Shoko.

SHOKO: Kamisama. The wind is picking up!

They exit. Genovevo is alone. For the first time perhaps ever, he seems to relax his shoulders. To settle into his reality.

GENOVEVO: *(a nod heavenward)* **Gracias.**

As he breathes eyes closed in silent thanks, --

"DAICHI" plays as The Yamadas return. Min is grey, sunken, changed. Ted looks great, better than ever. They survey the fields.

MIN: *(grunt meaning "wow")*

TED: Look at all them berries! *(a touch sad)* Guess they had a great year.

Arnulfo appears. Genovevo awakens. Watches in disbelief.

ARNULFO: *(approaching)* Ted, is that you?!! *(shakes their hands)* Glad you're back. *(to MIN)* You look...different.

MIN: *(grunts)*

ARNULFO: *(clueless)* So how was camp?

TED: *(closing the topic)* That's another story.

Arnulfo gives Min a cigar. Min sees Genovevo.

MIN: *(meaning "look")* Ted.

Complete SILENCE. Genovevo approaches.

GENOVEVO: Welcome home.

Offers his hand. Min takes it.

MIN: *(grunts)*

Genovevo reacts at how small and fragile Min has become.

TED: Ya done good.

GENOVEVO: *(to MIN and TED)* You must be tired.

Shoko appears. Stunned silence. Shoko goes inside. Pichuka remains.

GENOVEVO: She's just surprised.

TED: Have we changed that much?

Genovevo and Min go inside. Ted lights a cigarette.

ARNULFO: *(watching them)* This ain't gonna be pretty.

Arnulfo goes. Macias follows. Pichuka remains with Ted.

TED: Hello Dutchess. How ya doing?

PICHUKA: **Genki-des**.

TED: You speak Japanese?

PICHUKA: About as good as you speak hepcat.

TED: Do I know you?

PICHUKA: You could.

TED: You remind me of someone I relied on.

PICHUKA: You remind me of a guy with a bloody nose.

TED: Wow. I kicked the habit. That's about the only good thing that came outa camp. *(beat)* But if you happened to bring some—

PICHUKA: Be cool, fool.

TED: Gotta cigarette?

Pichuka gives him one. He puffs deep.

TED: Drugs! Ain't no drugs in Tule Lake. I went straight! Tried to join up—you know, the 442! *(their motto)* Go for broke! *(beat)* But the doctor said I got hepatitis. Not the kind of hepcat I intended. Not fit for military service. Not fit for much anymore. Enough to drive a man to drugs! *(laughs)* That was a joke.

PICHUKA: You don't look sick.

TED: Got one of those inscrutable faces.

PICHUKA: You got a nice face.

TED: You do too.

She takes the cigarette out of his mouth. Drags. They smoke in silence.

SCENE 7

Min wanders alone. Sees his kimono.

MIN: *(grunt meaning "still here?")* As he puts it on, --

Genovevo removes the deed. Shoko grabs Genovevo by the arm. They whisper heatedly.

GENOVEVO: This war had to end.

SHOKO: It's still going on!

GENOVEVO: I mean the one here. *(beat)* From that very first day, dreaming in the middle of the field, I felt like it was all pretend. Just a dream. Change your clothes, you can't change inside the clothes. You can't change— *(stops short)* You can't change.

SHOKO: What? Are you going to --?

GENOVEVO: Give it back.

SHOKO: How can you?

GENOVEVO: How can I not?

SHOKO: It's like giving a child away. Like giving away a part of your body --!

GENOVEVO: IT'S NOT MINE!

SHOKO: What about Arnulfo? And the **Braceros**? What are they supposed to do?

GENOVEVO: They can work for Min as easy as they worked for me.

SHOKO: You think that's all it is? Business? *(beat)* What about me?

GENOVEVO: I don't know.

SHOKO: Sell me back to Min for a dollar?

GENOVEVO: I didn't buy you.

SHOKO: I bought you.

GENOVEVO: What do you want me to do?!!

SHOKO: DON'T GIVE UP!!

GENOVEVO: What does that mean?!!

SHOKO: MAKE WAVES!! MAKE NOISE!!

GENOVEVO: I can't. *(she starts to go)* Don't go!

SHOKO: Why stay? I know how this movie ends.

GENOVEVO: Help me. *(beat)* In the movies, this is when you kiss me. And then I can do anything. *(kisses her passionately. She holds back)* Do you feel nothing?!!

SHOKO: I feel like I went to a movie in a language very foreign to me, very beautiful, with a very sad and handsome leading man. I'll always remember how he made me feel.

Min appears still in the kimono. Almost himself again.

MIN: Shoko!

Shoko exits.

MIN: Everytime she sees me she's gotta leave the room.

GENOVEVO: Give her time.

Min stares at Genovevo knowingly. Not so fragile anymore.

MIN: Show me the fields, wouldya? I think it's time we had a little talk.

Min sheds the kimono. They go outside to the fields.

SCENE 8

Sunset. THE FIELDS. "DAICHI" plays quietly.

MIN: *(grunts, then:)* I dreamed of this. And when they served strawberry jam? That was hard, almost couldn't eat it. They say you can't go home again.

GENOVEVO: I dreamed this too. You coming back. To take it all away.

MIN: How can I? I sold it. Plus I don't got all my rights back anyway.

GENOVEVO: Boss, --

MIN: You're the boss. What do they call it? The **patron**.

GENOVEVO: *(kicks the dirt)* We're both **patrones**.

MIN: How the hell ya gonna have two bosses?

GENOVEVO: This is terrible.

MIN: What can we do? There's this big pie, homemade and delicious. We oughta know, it's a strawberry pie! But it got tooken, right off the windowsill. By hook and by crook we found a way to hold onto a little sliver, for our families, for the child on the way. Just a little piece of pie. And I keep asking, I guess I'm stupid but I keep asking, why can't we have more pie?!! *(kicks the dirt)* I could buy it back from ya.

GENOVEVO: Things have changed.

MIN: Price gone up, has it?

GENOVEVO: Farm's a cooperative now, --

MIN: So cooperate with me.

GENOVEVO: Arnulfo and I made an agreement, --

MIN: So break it.

GENOVEVO: Just like that?

MIN: What kinda businessman are ya anyways? *(beat)* Look, okay okay. We'll honor your agreements. But first things first.

GENOVEVO: Then there's Shoko, --

MIN: Let's leave it lay where it comes to her. We're liable to get emotional, and this is business.

GENOVEVO: You have no claim anymore.

MIN: On her? You don't just walk away from a marriage license.

GENOVEVO: You did.

MIN: Heck, I thought I was going to one of them Hitler-style camps where you never come back. And her with her Japanese ways, they'd treat her worse than the rest of us. And they would've too! Look—marriage don't gotta be about love. It's about duty. And survival. We survived. That's a victory in itself. But duty calls. *(beat)* And as for this farm, you dumbassed Mickey, my father worked this land before either of us, and it was nothing but stone and rocks. But he broke 'em down, dug down deep and pulled each one out of the ground, turned this land into berries, and beans, and canteloupe, and all sorts of good things which wouldn'ta never been here without the sweat of his brow. And then he gave the damn thing to me. And Ted. He didn't give it to you.

GENOVEVO: *(staredown)* What do you want?

MIN: What do you want?

GENOVEVO: I don't want to have to choose.

MIN; That went the way of Santy Claus and the Tooth Fairy.

GENOVEVO: Then I want it all.

MIN: So do I. *(beat)* Start with the farm. Make the offer.

GENOVEVO: Chapos cabrones!

MIN: I thought you were an honorable man.

Genovevo gives Min the deed.

GENOVEVO: Take it. Every dream I ever had.

MIN: What about my dreams?

GENOVEVO: I hope they blow up in your face!

MIN: Don't talk to me like that!

Min grabs Genovevo. Genovevo shoves him off.

GENOVEVO: I'm not your slave.

Like two old warriors, each instinctively grabs a weapon. Min finds a short-handled hoe; Genovevo the long-handled one.

MIN: *(RE: the long handle)* New technology. *(twirls his like a sword)* But it ain't the size, it's what you do with it.

GENOVEVO: I don't want to fight. But I will. *(wields his like a machete)* Don't be stupid, Min.

MIN: I'm way past stupid.

GENOVEVO: Take the farm. Take Shoko. But treat me as a man, or I will kill you.

MIN: Don't take the moral highground with me! You screwed my wife! You bought the goddamn place for a lousy dollar!!

GENOVEVO: You're the **cabron** who sold it to me.

Min attacks. Genovevo responds. As metal hits metal and SPARKS fly, Shoko enters like a storm cloud. The others follow.

SHOKO: Stop it!!!

GENOVEVO: What are we supposed to do?

SHOKO: NOT THIS!!

MIN: Just getting back what's mine—

GENOVEVO: At what price?

SHOKO: Gimme a dollar.

MIN/GENOVEVO: What?

SHOKO: Gimme a dollar.

MIN/GENOVEVO: Me or him?

SHOKO: Both.

Both men fish for a dollar.

GENOVEVO: Price mighta gone up a bit.

SHOKO: That's why I'm taking two.

She takes the bills and TEARS them in half.

GENOVEVO: **Ay yi yi**.

MIN: I think that's illegal.

SHOKO: *(to MIN)* Don't look back. Don't lay blame—it never ends. Be free.

MIN: I don't know how.

SHOKO: You do.

She takes Min's hand. Genovevo misreads the meaning. Bears the total loss of every dream in SILENCE. CONJUNTO MUSICA begins.

ESQUINCLE: **A toda madre!!!** See I told you so!! Have your cake and eat it too!!! As he does the **taconazo**, the happy dance, in the fields—

MIN: What the hell is that?

GENOVEVO: *(grim)* Joy, I think.

MIN: Looks like he got a lizard up his pants!

GENOVEVO: That's what joy looks like. To be free. *(to SHOKO)* **Vaya don Dios**.

Genovevo retrieves his hat, walks off into the sunset. Shoko stops him.

SHOKO: *(to GENOVEVO)* And how it feels. *(takes his hand)* **Si Dios quiere**.

Genovevo and Min both stand in confusion.

SHOKO: *(to MIN)* Yamada? *(to GENOVEVO)* Llamada. I'm calling you. *(to both)* Let's get to work.

She breathes. Steps forward.

As Esquincle dances, --

CONJUNTO MUSICA sweeps us to—

END OF PLAY

Contributors

LUIS ALFARO's plays include *Straight as a Line, Bitter Homes and Gardens, Breakfast, Lunch and Dinner,* and *Electricidad*. His work as dramatist, performance artist and storyteller has been seen at Hartford Stage, Mark Taper Forum, Playwrights Arena, Primary Stages, Goodman Theatre, ICA, and many more. He was co-director of the Latino Theatre Initiative at the Mark Taper Forum Theatre (Center Theatre Group) for almost ten years. He has taught at, among other institutions, CalArts, UCLA, and USC. A MacArthur Fellow, he is the recipient of many awards and fellowships including an NEA/TCG Playwright in Residence at Borderlands Theatre in Arizona.

OLIVER MAYER is Assistant Professor of Dramatic Writing at USC School of Theatre. He is the author of *Blade to the Heat, Dark Matters, Conjunto, Dias y Flores, Rocio! In Spite of it All, Young Valiant, Joe Louis Blues, Joy of the Desolate, The Road to Los Angeles, Laws of Sympathy, The Righting Moment,* and *Bold as Love*. "The Hurt Business: A Critical Portfolio of the Early Works of Oliver Mayer" is published by Hyperbole Books. He wrote the libretto for *America Tropical*, a new opera composed by David Conte, which premiered this year in San Francisco. Screenplays include *Dare to Love Me* and *Blade to the Heat*. He is the recipient of a Gerbode Grant, a Sloan Initiative Commission, and a USC Zumberge Award for his work.

JON D. ROSSINI is an Assistant Professor in the Department of Theatre and Dance at the University of California, Davis. He has published articles in *American Drama, Gestos,* and *Journal of American Drama and Theater*, and has chapters in collections including *Codifying the Nation* and *Mediating Chicana/o Culture*. His book *Contemporary Latina/o Theater: Wrighting Ethnicity* is forthcoming from Southern Illinois University Press.

More Titles from

NoPassport Press
Dreaming the Americas Series

Lorca: Major Plays Volume I (Blood Wedding, Yerma, and The House of Bernarda Alba) translated by Caridad Svich

Lorca: Major Plays Volume II (The Shoemaker's Prodigious Wife, The Public, and Dona Rosita) translated by Caridad Svich

Anne Garcia-Romero: Collected Plays (Santa Concepcion, Earthquake Chica, and Mary Peabody in Cuba)

Alejandro Morales: Collected Plays (sebastian, expat/inferno, and marea)

NoPassport Press

PO Box 1786

South Gate CA 90280 USA

e-mail: NoPassportPress@aol.com

Breinigsville, PA USA
03 October 2010
246558BV00001B/37/P